acrossTOWN
Stories of Columbus

Proudly Presented By
COLUMBUS CREATIVE COOPERATIVE

Edited By
Amy S. Dalrymple, Brad Pauquette
& Kim Younkin

Pauquette ltd
dba Columbus Creative Cooperative
1658 Harvard Ave.
Columbus, OH 43203
www.ColumbusCoop.org

DEVELOPMENTAL EDITORS
Amy S. Dalrymple & Brad Pauquette

COPY EDITOR
Kim Younkin

PRODUCTION EDITOR
Brad Pauquette

PROOFREADER
Mallory Baker

All twelve stories included in this work are previously
unpublished.

Cover photograph by Melissa Pauquette, 2011.
Printed with permission.
MelissaPauquettePhotography.com

ISBN 978-0-9835205-3-5

Printed in the United States of America
1 3 5 7 9 10 8 6 4 2

CONTENTS

INTRODUCTION

I have a secret to tell you. It's more of a confession, really. Okay, it's a secret confession.

I love Columbus, Ohio.

I love the people, I love the local breweries and the farmers' markets, I love that we get four real seasons—hot in the summer and snowy in the winter. I get tingly all over just thinking about it.

Columbus is large enough to offer the amenities of a major metropolis, but small enough that you can still drive from one side to the other in 25 minutes. It's a truly amazing thing.

In 2008, my wife and I quit our jobs, sold everything we owned, and traveled the country in our Chevy Cavalier. We spent time in dozens of cities across the USA, from Pensacola to San Diego, Salt Lake City to Cedar Rapids. By the end of our wandering we realized, there's no place quite like Columbus, Ohio. It's the perfect average of America.

In Columbus, things don't move quite so slowly as they do in Mobile, Alabama, but we don't have the commotion and congestion of Southern California either. We might not have the sunny days and extreme weather of Denver, but we get a lot more variety in the skies than Seattle does.

We have two professional sports teams that compete on a national level, the corporate offices of a dozen or more multinational companies, and a large enough population that there's a group or organization for every niche interest, hobby or fetish imaginable.

Every story in this book is set in Columbus. You'll find that not every author has quite the amour for our burgeoning municipality as I do, but I'm certain that you'll be delighted with each unique story.

Not only is every story set in Columbus, but the collection you're holding in your hands right now is also written exclusively by authors who live and work in beautiful Central Ohio. These are people that you see every day—your bank teller, your waiter, your kid's teacher and your web designer.

We've assembled a fantastic variety of stories, with genres ranging from romantic comedy to science fiction, adventure to drama, crime to the supernatural, and every mix between.

I am confident that you will enjoy your time with this book.

When you purchase a Columbus Creative Cooperative anthology, you're not only getting a great piece of entertainment, but you're also supporting local art. Every book that sells is a pat on the back that tells these twelve writers, *what you're doing is important. Those hours you spent pecking away at your computer keyboard in the dark weren't a waste of time.*

So thank you. Thank you for purchasing our book. Thank you for supporting the written-word artists of Columbus. You, the reader, add so much value to our efforts.

Now you know my secret. But please...if my wife asks, Columbus and I are just friends.

-Brad Pauquette

Director, Columbus Creative Cooperative

For more information about Columbus Creative Cooperative, please visit **ColumbusCoop.org**.

Amy S. Dalrymple

Amy S. Dalrymple is originally from Milwaukee, Wisconsin and now lives in Columbus. She is pleased with Columbus's ample substitutes for Milwaukee's famed brews, however, she has yet to find a suitable replacement for good old Wisconsin cheese. Currently, she is going through an Irish Cheddar phase.

Amy doesn't have a favorite place to write, but, she enjoys wandering among Columbus' many coffee shops and has been spotted in up to three different coffee shops in one day. She sometimes switches to bars when she gets the shakes from too much coffee. She discovered by accident that the white noise of a loud bar on a weeknight is conducive to writing. She prefers well-worn Moleskine notebooks and felt ink pens to laptops, and she carries both with her at all times in case of sudden inspiration.

"A Good Day for a Walk" is a work of fiction, but some parts of the story were inspired by Amy's time as a barista, which ranks as one of her favorite jobs.

Amy would like to extend special gratitude to Ben Caplan and Amanda Comstock for their assistance with the French language portions of this story. Any remaining mistakes are her own.

To learn more about Amy's work and upcoming projects, please visit www.amydalrymple.com.

A GOOD DAY FOR A WALK
By Amy S. Dalrymple

Four a.m. A blaring alarm jerks me from peaceful slumber. Vague memories of pleasant dreams dissipate with the *Errr-Err-Err-Err*-ing, and I briefly consider calling off. This is the best night of sleep I've had in ages. Endless months of insomnia, of restless wandering through my one-bedroom apartment, of early evening runs to the corner store for Diet Dr. Pepper, and late night jogs through the vacant Bexley streets. I run past quiet mansions, where maybe all is not well, but at least the inhabitants can afford prescription sleeping pills. The doctor says it's a side effect of the illness, an illness I still can't name or admit to.

I backhand the top of the alarm clock, but by the time the blaring stops, it's too late. I stumble out of bed—well, to be honest, just a twin size mattress centered on a hand-me-down rag rug. The best I can do with the earnings from my part-time job just a hair above minimum wage.

I hold onto the walls and door frames on my way to the bathroom—I black out easily—where I try in vain to do something about my bloodshot eyes. Cold water, no time for cucumbers. Concealer to try to hide the dark circles underneath. I comb my bangs across my forehead, trying to cover up as much of my face as I can. I'm far too pale for most makeup, I always look like a botched spray-tan job—orange. It's not my color.

Still in my pajamas, I step out the back door to determine the temperature. Frigid December air jolts me awake, and immediately I can see my breath escaping as a thick cloud. I slam the door behind me and scamper around in search of layers.

Lately, I can't stay warm no matter what I do, and as the days grow shorter and colder and more brutal, I add more and more layers of clothing. My jeans and khaki work pants are getting baggier, which means I have room for leggings underneath, and knee socks, and then leg warmers if I need them, in aqua and magenta. Back to the '80s for me, which

5

should be motivation enough to put on some weight. On top, two camis and a long-sleeve thermal, then a black polo shirt, black cardigan. Finally, my trusty trench coat, hat, scarf, and mittens.

Getting undressed is not so hard. Some nights, I don't even bother. Some nights, I just sort of collapse on the living room floor, not unconscious, really—for that I would be grateful—just *unmovable*. As the kitchen clock ticks away the minutes and then the hours, as I watch the gray skies fade to black through the drawn curtains of my front window, I sometimes wonder, what if I died?

Sometimes days and days go by, and no one calls. How long would it take for someone to notice? Someone other than my cat, Marcel, who pesters me with licks and meows, noticing that something is awry. Or maybe he's just hungry again.

But, lying there on the hardwood floor as if I am the only soul in the universe, I think, maybe the doctor's right. Maybe I am dying.

5:05 a.m. "You want a shot?" Grace asks, but she is grinding the espresso before I can reply.

No one eats breakfast at this ungodly hour. We usually start our morning with shots of espresso, straight out of porcelain demitasses, no cream. Grace likes to start slowly, but not me. I'll pull three shots if I get to the bar first, but Grace starts me off with a *doppio*. She hands me the demitasse, and we both drink together in silence. I'm rinsing my cup when she asks, "So, are you coming to the potluck?"

"Oh, I don't know...," I trail off, and my face feels warm because she's put me on the spot. "I'll try. I might have to babysit."

I feel bad for lying, because Grace hand-made invitations for everyone, and because I like my new coworkers, and because it's been a long time since I've been invited out—the first time since I had to drop out of art school. But I can't handle another party centered around food. Not this time of year.

"Well, I hope you can make it." She smiles and disappears

around back to open the safe. I begin opening the bar, where I will stay after we open, because I'm the fastest.

5:25. The coffee freaks are lining up outside the door, like die-hard fans waiting for tickets to a concert that won't sell out. I don't know why they don't just wait in their cars until we open. It annoys Grace, who hides in the back so she doesn't have to stare awkwardly at them through the picture windows, but I don't care. I like them.

5:30. I open the door, and the early birds pour in with bright red ears, rubbing their hands together. In another part of town, they would be lined up in the drive-thru, warm and cozy in their Lexuses and Priuses, but drive-thrus aren't allowed in Bexley, so they have to stumble inside, bleary-eyed and sometimes cranky, but always grateful. They tip well.

Grace emerges from the back to run the register, and I'm envious as always, because she appears so *normal*, so *healthy* at this hour—dusky blond hair pulled back into an elegant twist, bright eyes sans redness, sans circles, coral-colored lips creased into a smile. I'm thankful she allows me to hide behind the bar, where I can conceal my puffy eyes and pale skin and trembling hands, save for when I lean over the bar to call out drinks.

7:40. During a lull in the rush, a woman I don't recognize ambles in the door, calm and bright-eyed, as if she doesn't even need coffee. She looks like the kind of woman you could confide in. Chunky sweater, loose brown ponytail, comfortable flats.

"Good morning!" Grace says. "What can we get for you?"

"Cappuccino, extra-dry," she orders, and immediately I cringe. If the early birds are generally low-maintenance—Breakfast Blends, red-eyes, black-eyes—the cappuccino people are at the other end of the spectrum.

Cappuccino—it's such a difficult concept. To the purists, the people who think that only Italians can make true espresso, a cappuccino is no more than five to six ounces, mostly espresso and foam. They consider it a heinous crime to make a cappuccino any way but the Italian way, but they forget about pizza and its thousands of scrumptious permutations, probably none of them really *Italian*. Americans aren't the first or last people to adulterate cuisine. We're all nomads, and our food has always changed as we've walked wearily across the continents.

It's taken me months and months to master the steam wand, and I'm so proud when I have the chance to hand over a near-perfect cappuccino—a *moving* thing, dark, earth-colored crema swirled with lighter caramel-brown, topped with pure white foam, and served in porcelain.

When someone orders a "dry" cappuccino, it's usually safe to assume they want more than half foam. For "extra dry," basically all foam. But it's kind of like defining a color. What is cornflower blue, or periwinkle, or azure?

She complains nicely the first time. "Honey, there's a little more milk than I'm used to. Could you remake it?"

I do, but my hands are shaking already. Is it the three shots of espresso or anxiety or hunger? I can never tell. I feel the aluminum milk pitcher *clinking* and *clanging* against the steam wand; I feel burning eyes on me; I feel my cheeks flush with rare color. I place the cappuccino on the hand-off station without a word.

This time, her kindness dissipates. "Honey, there's still a lot of milk, and it's a four-dollar drink."

I no longer feel like confiding in her. I feel like inviting her behind the bar to do a better damn job herself. I feel like throwing the drink across the gray slate floor, ruining both my cumulus foam and her comfortable flats.

Instead, I dump the rejected cappuccino into the stainless steel sink behind the bar and run to Grace. Without a word, I hand her the paper cup and take her place at the register. She understands and walks to the bar, pours a fresh pitcher of milk, and begins to steam it.

I'm not as tough as I try to be. I fight back tears as I ring up the next customer. After Grace finally rids us of Extra Dry Cappuccino, she says, "I'm sorry. You can take a break as soon as Matt gets here. He shouldn't be more than a few minutes."

I nod.

It *is* more than a few minutes, but finally, Matt arrives, and

I ring up the last customer before I can escape to the back. It's Thomas, a regular, whose son Josh works here, too. He doesn't have to order—he always drinks Breakfast Blend, no room for cream. He hands me his credit card with a smile.

"I'll pay for him, too," he says, and nods toward the man behind him. Dark hair, dark eyes, a scruffy three-day beard, maybe thirty-five. Dressed mostly in black, with a bright, cashmere scarf peeking through his overcoat. Azure.

"Antoine. He's visiting from France. Josh met him on a train when he backpacked across Europe after high school."

"Welcome." I do my best to sound cheerful, though there is still a lump in my throat.

Antoine gives me a shy smile.

"And for you?"

He speaks to me quickly in a language I don't know. French. I look helplessly for Thomas, but he's nowhere to be found. I have nothing to say to him in his own language, so, I speak English.

"What can I get for you?" I ask, hoping he can pick up a few clues from my tone. "Coffee?" I try, and I point to the three stacks of cups to my right, displaying the sizes.

"No—thank you." He gazes for a moment at our menu and then proceeds with a long string of words I don't understand— fast and so beautiful that I stop everything to listen, nearly forgetting that I'm trying to do a job, trying to take an order, that there is a small line accumulating behind him.

"Latte? Tea?"

He shrugs and says, "*Doppio*," and then I smile—a real smile—for the first time all morning, or maybe all week. I don't speak French, and he doesn't speak English, but at least we both know a little Italian.

I swipe Thomas's credit card and return it to Antoine with a smile that says: "Please, stay awhile. I'm a foreigner here, too."

Failing to read my mind, he just says, "Thank you," drops a couple of bills in the tip jar, and leaves the counter in search of his espresso.

Matt taps me on the shoulder, and I've never been so happy

to see him. I've nearly made my escape when I hear someone calling out, *"Excusez-moi!"* and I see Antoine across the counter. I walk around to the other side, and he's right in front of me, and before I can take a step back for comfort, he takes my right hand and places two Euro coins in it.

"Thank you," he says, carefully, then turns and leaves through the front door. The warmth of his touch lingers as I wander to the back for my break.

I took Spanish in high school, because it seemed the most likely language to be useful. My French is limited to what I've been able to pick up from *Amelie*, and a handful of Audrey Tautou's other films—which is to say, very little.

But after work, I'm still enamored of Antoine. His presence today almost cured me of my ill humor, and though I usually trudge home slowly, my feet heavy and my bones aching long before the sun has even thought of setting, today there is a little spring to my step.

Most afternoons after work, I drape myself across the sofa, or my barren mattress, or the hardwood floor, waiting until I can shore up enough strength to take a hot shower, or to try to wake myself up with hot tea. But today I jump in the shower right away and change into a fresh set of about nine layers. When my hair seems dry enough to leave the house, I dash across the street to the bus stop—the #2, East Main to Downtown. I hop off at Main and Grant and walk briskly the rest of the way to the main library.

I sign out a computer and search for an English-French translation website that seems reliable. I only have the computer for one hour, so as quickly as possible, I write out useful phrases, followed by phonetic pronunciations.

Later, back in the privacy of my apartment, I practice saying them out loud.

"Je m'appelle Lucy," I say to Marcel.

He doesn't look impressed. I worry that I have mispronounced my own name.

Next, I try something simpler: *"Vouz désirez?"* What

would you like?

It sounds all wrong. I need a second opinion. I call my little sister, who I had advised to take high school Spanish and who signed up for French instead, probably because she knows it's best to consider my advice and then do the opposite.

"I'm glad you decided to take French," I tell her. "I need some help with my pronunciation."

"Why?" she asks, sounding a little annoyed. "And since when do you study French?"

I tell her about Antoine.

"Okay, since it's for a guy. But we have to make it fast. I'm dyeing my hair."

She seems to be dyeing her hair every time I call, but I decide not to harass her about it. I scribble notes into my Moleskine while we talk, and after I get off the phone with her, I transfer all my new newly acquired French phrases onto one fluorescent green note card, front and back.

The next morning, 4 a.m. The alarm jars me from another nearly sleepless night, this one somehow even worse than the last. I splash cold water on my face. I splash warm water on my face. Still, I look like death.

At work, I beat Grace to the bar, and I pull myself three shots of espresso. Eventually, I wake up enough to surreptitiously study my note card between customers.

Antoine arrives for his coffee during a rush. He's dressed in black again, but today his scarf is bright orange. I'm at the bar, six drinks behind, and when I see him out of the corner of my eye, all my French leaves me. I, who can barely speak English without stuttering—why have I been so foolish to believe I could speak a language I don't know to a stranger?

A line of customers gathers behind him, and they all seem to be watching. After a moment, the phrases I've memorized come back to me, but my heart is beating fast, and I realize with great disappointment that I've lost my nerve.

Then, spontaneously, just before he turns to walk away, I say, *"Bonjour!"*

11

My cheeks flush, but I see a smile spread quickly across his face.

He replies, with equal hesitance, "Have a good day."

Suddenly, I feel better. For a fleeting moment, the gap has closed, the wide and jagged chasm that separates me from everyone else has closed.

A few hours later, I'm clocking out for my lunch break when I overhear Grace and Matt talking about Antoine.

"Josh said he's leaving this afternoon," Matt says.

"Today?!" I repeat, with a little more emotion than I intended.

"Someone has a crush," Matt teases.

"No, no I don't have a crush," I say, but my cheeks feel a little warm, and Matt shakes his head. I walk away, shoulders slumped. I've lost my chance, forever, to get to know Antoine, and I feel a strange and unexpected sadness because of it. I've wiled away so many nights alone in my barren apartment, wanting nothing more than conversation, never brave enough to reach out my hand or to walk out my front door. But now Antoine is leaving, now I can see that I'm missing out on something good.

I only have thirty minutes for lunch, and I haven't brought anything to eat. I never do. Even if I could summon the courage, I could never bear to eat in front of them—my coworkers. But today seems different. Today, I said *bonjour* to a stranger, and today the sun is streaming through fluffy clouds from bright blue skies, uncommonly warm for this late in the year. Today, maybe I can eat a sandwich.

I can't bear to plan ahead, to premeditate this or any other meal, so I just start walking. I'm surprised not to be shivering as usual, and I'm sweating by the time I step into Aladdin's. I order a chicken shawarma rolled pita and wolf it down while walking back to work. The food brings me quickly back to life—my head stops spinning, and my nail beds slowly turn from blue to pink.

I'm not the only one to savor this unexpectedly warm day—several customers have taken their coffee out to the front patio. I'm pulling open the door to let myself back inside when I notice Antoine sitting alone at a table near the front of the building.

Without allowing myself the privilege of anxiety, I run inside to the back room, retrieve my fluorescent green note card, and meet Antoine at his table, slightly out of breath.

Suddenly it occurs to me that the phrases I had memorized left little room to ease gracefully into conversation.

"I-I-I-I'm sorry," I stutter. I was not clever enough to look up this phrase that is so necessary to me in English.

"*Comment allez-vous?*" I try. How are you? But my words come out mangled, and Antoine looks at me as if I'd just asked him to remove his shoe and eat it.

"*Je parle*—" I stop, make a generic hand sign for little, "—*français.*"

He laughs, kindly, quietly. He uses a similar improvised sign language to show me that he understands.

"A little," he repeats. "*Un peu.*"

His warmth allows me the confidence to continue.

"*Je m'appelle Lucy?*" I say. It's more a question than a statement: do you understand?

He does.

"*Je m'appelle Antoine,*" he replies.

"Antoine?" I repeat.

He nods and says something that was not on my note card.

"*C'est une belle journee pour prendre une marche.*"

He translates, "It's a good day for a walk."

Antoine's English is just as shaky as my French. He repeats the French again and waits for me. I force only one syllable out before my voice falters. But he is patient. He says the words slowly and clearly, and this time, I finish the entire sentence.

"*C'est une belle journee pour prendre une marche.*"

He's right; it is a good day. The sun is beating down on us as if it is still early autumn, and although I know it is fleeting, I smile, I forget my fears of winter, of the bitter cold that sinks into my skin, into my lungs, into my bones, threatening to take me out. For though I can't admit what I've done to my own body, I know that the cold will get me, that I'm one bad virus away from a hospital visit I can't pay for. *So*, I think, *I'll enjoy it. I'll just enjoy this moment.*

I begin to forget my fears, and we continue talking even after I've used up all of the phrases on my note card. We use broken English and broken French, improvised sign language and hesitant gestures, tone of voice, and awkward laughter.

He tells me he is from a town twenty kilometers outside Paris and that he is flying home later that day, by way of New York City. He is thirty-six, and he is single. He works at a boring job in a boring office—"*C'est ennuyeux*," he says, wrinkling his brow—and he doesn't know if he'll return. He hasn't ventured very far beyond the Continent until now.

"Why?" I ask, remembering after I say it that I have the question words on my note card. "*Pourquoi?*"

"*Je ne sais pas.*" He shrugs. But in his eyes I catch a glimmer of sadness, a look that I suspect my own eyes often belie. It's the reason I hide them. Behind the bar, behind my bangs, in the safety of my apartment.

"*Je voudrais...,*" I begin. I want...

What do I want?

I clasp my thumbs together in front of me, forming my hands into a bird. I want to fly away.

"*...a France.*" I haven't told anyone this before.

"*Oui,*" he smiles. "You will visit me?" He gestures for my note card, pulls a pen from his shirt pocket, and writes his name and email address.

I want to spend more time with him, but I see a flock of teenage girls headed our way for their ritual afternoon smoothies, and when I turn toward the door, Grace is waving me inside.

"I'm sorry," I say again in English, and I know he understands, but he won't teach me the French. "I have to go." I take his hand in my own with unfamiliar confidence and shake it firmly.

"It was nice to meet you."

"Nice to meet *you*," he says, and he rises, too.

"*Au revoir!*" I call out, waving as I run back inside, my heart still beating fast. And just as quickly as he hurried into my life, he is gone.

Not long afterward, I'm leaving, too. The spring in my step has weakened considerably since yesterday. The pita has worn off, and so has the thrill of my adventure. I'm halfway home when the church bells begin tolling, first the time—one o'clock—then an old hymn, one I recognize from my childhood but cannot name. Antoine's words echo in my mind, *c'est une belle journee pour prendre une marche,* and they remind me of the sun, which is still shining bright, and I remember that dusk is hours away, and that I can do anything I want with what remains of this one beautiful day.

Daniel O'Riordan

Daniel O'Riordan was born in Youngstown, Ohio, where he grew up on a beef and dairy farm. He attended Kent State University where he received a Bachelor's degree in Music with a minor in Secondary Education. After college, he owned and operated a small pizza shop in Northeastern Ohio and later worked at Vanderbilt University in Nashville, Tennessee.

He attended the Clarion Writers' Workshop at Michigan State University, a six-week writers' workshop often described as a boot camp for science fiction and fantasy writers. There he received instruction and feedback from authors and editors such as Tim Powers, Ellen Kushner, Karen Joy Fowler, Kate Wilhelm, Damon Knight, Gardner Dozois, and Gordon Van Gelder.

His publishing credits include sales to *Beyond...Science Fiction and Fantasy* and *Aboriginal Science Fiction*. He is currently working on a contemporary fantasy novel, *A Spark Awaiting*, set in Arizona and referencing Hopi mythology.

He now lives in Columbus, Ohio with his wife, Kathy, three dogs, and a not unreasonable number of ferrets.

KILLER
By Daniel O'Riordan

To Barney Jeffries, the sprawled bodies that littered the alley all looked like Michelle. Or, at least, the filthy, bullet-riddled remains he'd identified at the medical examiner's office. The residents of this byway that ran between Third Avenue and High Street in downtown Columbus, Ohio didn't even know he was there, lost in their bliss, high on Killer. He checked each Kreep against the photo Jack and Marge Stiverson gave him of their son. Johnny Stiverson wasn't here.

For about the hundredth time, he checked the S.I.G.'s heft in its shoulder holster. If a Kreep went Krazy, the nine millimeter was all that stood between him and an ugly death. It didn't fill him with a lot of comfort. He'd seen the police reports. It usually took a lot more than his two clips to bring down a Krazy, even at point-blank range.

To the right, the blank wall of the Rhodes Office Tower was free of blissed-out addicts and garbage. Building security for the state office tower did a good job driving off the Kreeps to keep their loading dock clear.

The other side of the alley hadn't fared so well. Killer addicts slumped against the boarded-up remains of businesses, a print shop and several restaurants, whose customers wouldn't risk running into a Kreep gone Krazy on a murderous rampage.

A scream echoed through the dim alley, and Barney compulsively grabbed the gun's textured grip. Probably not a Krazy. Folks nailed by those jokers didn't last long enough to scream.

The lowlifes must have caught someone. That wasn't good. You had to be pretty out there yourself to hang out in a shooting gallery, what with the slim pickings and the chance for an ugly death of your own. The nodding addicts ignored him as he took off at a run.

He skidded to a halt as he rounded a corner to a small side alley filled with trash. A young woman stood beside a dumpster trying to cover herself with her ripped clothing.

"Are you all right?" he asked.

She nodded as she pawed ineffectually at her blouse. Barney shrugged out of his suit jacket and put it around her shoulders. She pressed against him with great heaving sobs. He held her close and made soothing noises.

He noticed the bodies while he held her. Lowlifes, certainly, too clean to be Kreeps. One lay in a crumpled heap beside the dumpster while another sat against the far brick wall. His head lolled to the side, the ugly blotch on the wall above him suggested he wouldn't wake up again.

"What happened here?" he asked.

She glanced at the nearest body, then pulled his jacket tighter around herself. "They attacked me," she said in a shaky voice. "They were going to...well, you know. I screamed, but they didn't care. Said no one around here would notice.

"This man showed up, though. Told them to leave me alone. They went after him, but he was fast. I've never seen anyone that fast. One minute, they had me, the next, they were both like that." She gestured at one of the inert bodies.

Barney fished the picture of Johnny Stiverson out of his pocket. "This guy that helped you, this him?"

"Yeah," she said after studying the photo. "He's a lot dirtier than in that picture, but that's him. I think he heard you coming. He was making sure I was all right, then he jumped up on the dumpster and went from there up to the fire escape."

Well, he'd evidently found Johnny Stiverson. The description fit. So did his actions. He hadn't believed Marge Stiverson's claim that her son could control the Krazy mode, but there's no way a Kreep could do all he'd done otherwise. If he'd gone Krazy, though, there should be three bodies in this alley instead of two.

Gently disengaging himself from the woman, he pulled out his phone. "Let's get you some help," he said.

Barney took a long, hot shower as soon as he got home. He scrubbed until he was red and raw, but he still didn't feel clean. Something about spending so much time with those wasted lives seeped into him and couldn't be washed away.

Afterward, he settled into his chair with a cold beer and a picture of Michelle and Janet from happier times. Michelle was twelve when he'd snapped that photo at Lake Erie. That had been a good day. The perfect couple, Janet looked happier than anyone had a right to be, and, if he squinted just right, he could see Michelle's potential radiating out from her. She had her whole life ahead of her—a bright, confident girl who could do anything she wanted.

That was before the Killer. Before she sank down into that cesspool he'd spent the day in, doing things he didn't want to think about for money for the next high. It was probably a blessing the drug turned on her so quickly.

Less than six months after she ran away, Barney identified what was left of the body, literally ripped to shreds by a barrage of bullets to keep her from tearing the throat out of a lawyer on Gay Street—her fourth victim after going Krazy.

The Attorney General's children's fingerprint program had done its job. He didn't recognize what was left of her, and, without that, they might never have figured out who she was.

The funeral had been tough on Janet, tough on both of them, and all the joy they'd ever known went into that god-awful hole with their princess. Janet moved back to Dayton, her hometown, six months later.

He'd figured Johnny Stiverson for the same fate. It happened to all of them eventually, why should he be any different? Evidently, he was.

Jack and Marge Stiverson had Johnny fingerprinted at the A.G.'s booth at the state fair, so he ran those before he went out among the Kreeps. That didn't bring up any hits, and none of the Medical Examiner's John-Doe Krazies fit the kid's description. Kreeps never went into rehab voluntarily, so the chance little Johnny got himself clean was zilch.

The kid should still be out there in one of the galleries.

Of course, today hadn't been a total waste. The woman in the alley, Amy Whitehouse, confirmed the area where Johnny hung out. It also told him the boy could be drawn out by

19

someone in trouble. He could use that. If Johnny Stiverson felt the need to rescue damsels in distress, Barney could give him one.

Barney couldn't find anyone who'd take his offer to act as bait for Johnny Stiverson. There wasn't enough money in the world to entice most people down into that twilight world. Fortunately, he didn't need cooperation from any of the contacts he'd developed over the years. The alleys held a ready supply of Kreeps who'd do just about anything for money. He had breakfast at the Tim Horton's at Broad and High, then headed up to the alley that ran from Broad down to Gay Street where Amy had been rescued. He wanted to find a willing Kreep early before they all got the chance to fix.

Just past nine o'clock, it looked like he was already too late. Bodies littered the alley like the aftermath of some natural disaster, everyone dirty, unkempt, and oblivious. He finally came across a girl, maybe late teens or early twenties, who looked more alert than anyone around her.

Barney sucked in a surprised breath when he checked her out. Lank, tangled hair hung down in her eyes, blonde perhaps but so matted with dirt it was hard to say. That's what got him. Her hair looked just like Michelle's, minus the blood, of course, when he'd identified her.

The eyes cemented the impression. They didn't have the blank emptiness the Kreeps off in la-la land exhibited. There was alertness there, a clear blue, so much like Michelle's before she'd run off. Before...

She radiated suspicion as Barney approached. Her arms hung at her sides, impossibly thin and a testament to the lousy nutrition common to Kreeps. She didn't move, but she angled her head to watch him.

"Want to make a quick twenty?" Barney asked.

"For what?" the Kreep asked. Barney doubted he was the first to ask her that question.

"Nothing too serious," Barney answered. "I need you to scream at the top of your lungs for a couple of minutes."

20

"And that gets me twenty?"

Barney pulled a bill out of his pocket and held it out. The Kreep's eyes lit up.

"Anything special I should scream?" she asked.

Barney shrugged. "I don't know. 'No, stop, please help me.' That sort of thing."

The Kreep took a deep breath, then let loose. A blood-curdling scream bounced off the alley walls. None of the other Kreeps noticed.

"Oh, God, no!" she yelled. "Please, stop! Oh, God, help me, someone! Please!"

She kept it up for a full two minutes. Barney watched around them, his hand on his nine millimeter, while the Kreep yelled her head off. After she stopped, Barney tossed her the twenty. She leveraged herself to her feet to stumble off in search of a dealer. Barney hoped she didn't go Krazy. He didn't want that on his conscience. A gentle scraping behind him brought him around with his gun out.

Johnny Stiverson stood ten feet away. Barney couldn't tell if the kid was straight or high.

"Hold on," he said. "I just want to talk. Don't do anything crazy."

Johnny laughed. "Crazy, eh? With a C or a K?"

"You know what I mean."

The kid looked around. "Someone screamed. Where is she?"

"Off getting high. I gave her twenty for that performance."

"Any special reason?"

"To get you here," Barney said. "So I could talk to you."

Johnny shrugged. "You pretty much killed my high. What do you want?"

"Your parents sent me. They're worried sick about you. They want you home. I bet they'd even pay for rehab. You could get straightened out and lead a normal life."

The kid laughed again. "Dear mommy and daddy. What makes you or them think I want to get straight? Do you know how incredible this stuff is?"

21

Barney shook his head. "Can't say that I do. They hired me to find you, though. Paid good money for my services. That should count for something, shouldn't it?"

"They wasted their money. I can do such amazing things when I'm not buzzing. Why would I want to give that up just to be normal?"

Barney gestured at the dirty, sprawled bodies everywhere, fast food wrappers and other trash scattered among them. "You can't mean to say you like this?"

"You don't understand, and I can't explain it to you. You'd have to see the world like I do first."

"Fat chance of that."

Johnny came at him in a blurred motion that took Barney by surprise. In the time it took for his heart to skip a beat, the kid stood nose to nose with him, his right hand wrapped around Barney's throat while he clamped Barney's gun hand in a steel grip. Bright sparks filled Barney's vision while his arm went numb. The S.I.G. dropped to the alley floor.

"Get out of here," Johnny said, "and don't come back."

He pushed Barney away so he bounced off the rough wall behind him. Barney's knees gave out as he cracked his head against the wall. He dropped to all fours while throbbing pain slammed through his skull.

The S.I.G. was Barney's first thought, and he lunged forward to grab it. He came up on his knees with the gun pointing toward Johnny Stiverson.

But Barney and the Kreeps had the place to themselves.

The place didn't look any different a day later. The Kreeps were still there, lost in their pleasure, and trash was everywhere. From the looks on their faces, Jack and Marge Stiverson cycled back and forth between horror and disgust. He could sympathize. The anguish that threatened to pour his lunch all over the morgue floor when he identified Michelle's remains fought with the shock that filled him at the sight of what his daughter had become. The cute little girl he'd played with in the Park of Roses disappeared the moment she snuck out while they slept.

The first time he'd set foot in one of these alleys looking for Johnny Stiverson, all he could think about was his little girl in a place like this. What had her life truly been like? Was the drug that good, or her life before it that bad? The Stiversons were just starting the process.

"This is where you saw him?" Marge asked.

"Yeah," Barney answered. He gestured at the dumpster. "Right over there."

"And, he looked like these...things?" Jack Stiverson asked.

Barney nodded. "More alert, but pretty much the same. Dirty, thin. You know."

Jack couldn't take his eyes off the nearest Kreep, blissed out. "You think he's still around?"

"It's a safe bet. Kreeps don't usually stray that far from their home turf. They know where the best handouts are, the local dealers. That's all they care about."

"So, Mr. Jeffries," Marge said, "how do we find him?"

"Call him. He's fast and strong, and he can hear like nobody's business. You call his name, and he'll hear you."

"And he'll come?"

Barney looked away. He'd had that hope, too, the belief Michelle would just walk back through the door, and everything would be fine. That hope had been slapped down, and it destroyed everything that was important to him. It could happen in the next few minutes to Marge Stiverson, and he didn't relish being a witness to it.

"I don't know," he finally said. "It's all I could think of. He won't come for me again. Maybe he'll listen to you."

"Johnny!" she yelled. "Johnny! It's Mom. Dad's here, too. Please. We need to see you."

Barney pivoted around to watch on all sides for Johnny Stiverson. The alley remained peacefully quiet, the Kreeps ignoring them while the sounds of traffic floated down from Gay Street.

"What the hell are *they* doing here?"

Johnny Stiverson stood beside the dumpster, the same place

Barney first saw him yesterday. Before any of them could react, he crossed to snatch Barney by the throat again.

"What did you do?" he demanded. "What gives you the right?"

"They had to see you," Barney gasped. "They want to help you. Just accept it."

"You need to get out of here," he said to Marge. "It isn't safe. This idiot can't protect you."

Marge stepped up to put a hesitant hand on his arm. The boy's whole body quivered and the movement caused more pressure on Barney's neck. He scrabbled at the hand clamped there, but it was like slapping a steel post.

A scream he'd feared and expected since the first time Barney set foot in one of these damned alleys echoed off the blank walls. The grip on his neck slackened.

Shit, Barney thought, *not now.*

Down by a thick steel door, a Kreep around Johnny's age lurched to his feet. He grabbed his head as he hunched over and screamed again. Not many people heard that and lived to describe it.

The Krazy reached for a nearby Kreep still in the throes of his high. "Help me, goddammit!" he yelled.

The Kreep ignored him, and the Krazy grabbed the other junkie by the arm to yank him up. That still didn't rouse the kid. The Krazy jerked him around, and the kid's arm snapped off, blood spewing from the stump to paint the wall with gore. The kid's screams rivaled the Krazy's. A moment later, the Krazy lifted the helpless boy off his feet and hurled him across the alley to slam into the opposite wall. The poor kid dropped to the ground in a heap, the blood and screaming both cut off in an abrupt moment.

Barney pulled out his gun. It looked and felt puny compared to the power he'd just witnessed.

"Get out of here!" he yelled at the Stiversons. They didn't argue with him. They headed up the alley at a run.

Johnny rushed to the Krazy. The kid looked up as Johnny barreled down on him. He held out his hands as if begging.

"Make it stop!" he pleaded. "There's hornets buzzing in my brain! Make them go away."

Johnny wrapped his arms around the kid's head. With a concrete grip, Johnny jerked the Krazy's head around. The sharp crack of the broken neck reached Barney across the alley. The Krazy convulsed, then hung loosely in Johnny's grip. Johnny let go, and the Krazy dropped to the alley floor like a marionette with cut strings.

Johnny crossed the distance to Barney with another blurred motion. They did their previous dance, with one hand wrapped around Barney's neck while the other immobilized his S.I.G.

"What were you thinking, bringing my parents down here? Do you want to get them killed? What? You thought that would make me see the error of my ways and come with you to rehab? You stupid, stupid old man! You want to know what you're dealing with? Come on."

Johnny squeezed Barney's wrist, and his hand went numb. The grip remained around his neck, but Johnny let go of Barney's wrist to snatch the gun out of midair. He slid it into his waistband.

Then, he transferred his hold from Barney's neck to his arm so he could drag him along. Barney had no choice but to follow.

Johnny jumped up on the dumpster with a light hop. Barney went with him. From there, Johnny grabbed the lower rungs of the fire escape ladder, a good ten feet above the dumpster. Barney dangled from the kid's grip while he climbed one-handed up to the lowest platform.

Johnny took the metal steps two at a time at a speed that barely gave Barney the chance to get his feet under him. They went up, all the way to the top, so fast Barney was afraid he'd lose his breakfast.

At the top, Johnny tossed him over the balustrade where he landed in a heap in the light gravel coating strewn across the roof. Barney tried to get his feet under him while Johnny jumped over the barrier to land beside him. He wasn't even breathing hard.

"Not bad, eh?" Johnny said. "Pretty damned impressive,

if you ask me. I just carried your fat ass up five flights at a run."
He held his arms out to his sides. "Look at me. Not winded in
the least. I bet you can't get up in the middle of the night to take
a piss without breaking a sweat."

"Which is why you should go to the Army," Barney
croaked. His throat still hurt. "That's what they designed that
stuff for. If they could make it work, you'd be doing the country
a big service. You'd be a hero. A patriot."

"What do you care?"

"My daughter got on that shit. Went Krazy in no time. You
know what the police do with Krazies."

Johnny looked down at the rooftop while he scuffed the
gravel with a well-worn tennis shoe. "Sorry," he said.

"I could almost convince myself her death meant something
if just one of you hopheads figured out how to make everything
work so our soldiers don't get killed in battle. You're it. Like it
or not, Stiverson, you're the only thing that can redeem all the
dying this crap's responsible for."

"Don't lay that on me, old man. You don't know what
you're talking about. I just wanted to make sure the Kreeps
enjoyed their highs without getting hassled."

"But, Michelle, my daughter—"

"Your daughter's dead! You want to know how many other
daughters would be dead if I gave this to the Army?"

He pointed at the Atlas Building, two blocks away. "See
the top floor, third window from the right? The guy there just
jammed the copier up something fierce. You want to know what
he's saying? I can read lips now. You can probably guess. It
isn't very original."

Johnny pointed in the other direction. "And Broad Street.
I can tell you the make and model of every car down there by
its engine sound. You saw what it took to haul you up here.
Nothing. And you want to give this to some idiot with a gun?
Krazies do some serious damage, but it's always limited because
it's mindless. Imagine a Krazy with a gun and his wits. He'd
wipe out every living thing in whatever hellhole they dropped
him into."

"He'd have training," Barney said. "That would keep him in check."

Johnny laughed. "How do you train a god not to use his power against insects? That's what it would be like. Go home, old man."

Barney slowly climbed to his feet. "The name's Barney," he said. "Barney Jeffries."

The S.I.G. landed at Barney's feet. "Go home, Barney. Go tell my parents you saw me fighting the Krazy before you took off to save yourself. Tell them you don't know what happened to me. And don't come down here again. It isn't safe."

"That's it? Just pretend none of this happened? What about my daughter? What about her death? You saying it was all for nothing?"

"Every Krazy's death is for nothing."

Johnny ran toward the edge of the roof. With a hop, he soared across the gap to the next building. He landed with his legs pumping, crossed that building in seconds, and arched up and away toward the next rooftop. In moments, he was gone. Barney picked up his gun before he walked to the edge and looked down at the fire escape. He looked back at the rooftop. It was empty.

Michelle was gone, so was Johnny, and Barney had a nasty trek down ahead of him. He climbed over the roof edge to the fire escape and started back to the alley floor, where the Kreeps lay sprawled.

Gabrielle Gold

Writing fantasy fiction, poems, and songs has been a part of Gabrielle Gold's life since the third grade, when she wrote a forty-two page story purely for her own enjoyment.

At Ohio Wesleyan University, where she earned her B.A. in Medieval Studies, she contributed multiple times to *Confiscated*, a student-run literary magazine. She also won third place in the university's 2006 Global Outreach Talent Show, an intercollegiate contest that raised money for the humanitarian effort in Darfur. After she graduated, she went on to complete her M.A. in Art History. Defying the initial skepticism of her advisor, she successfully completed her master's thesis on the symbolism of bears in medieval German and Swiss art.

Aside from her accomplishments within the academic sphere, Gabrielle Gold has been a loyal member of the Columbus arts community since high school. She won first place in the 2004 songwriting contest at Marcon. This past October, she attended a local music convention known as the Ohio Valley Filk Festival for the fifth time, and is hoping to start her own Columbus filk music circle.

The story in this anthology is Gabrielle Gold's first published work of fiction. She is currently editing a draft of one fantasy novel and has several others in the works. She lives in Upper Arlington, Ohio, with her brother and his two cats.

HIDDEN BRILLIANCE
By Gabrielle Gold

I have less than one month.

He flitted sideways, landing beside a thick trail of sap that leaked from a wound in the nearest banana tree, his thoughts swirling about like dust motes. Inserting his long proboscis into the hole, he drank deeply from its syrupy well. Although he relished the taste of the sap on his feet, something inside him beyond the desires of the insect was not sated. There was more, a task to be done. Fulfillment. And he had less than one month left.

Inácio knew his name when he emerged from the chrysalis eighty-five days ago, struggling to free his weak and trembling wings from each other and the sticky mass that bound them. He recalled the time when he was given this name, when he could watch the sun rise while cradling his wife's head in his arm. He remembered the sound of voices only faintly, as an abstract concept, like God or the size of the universe. All of this knowledge of days gone by weighed heavily on his fragile body. The urgent sense that he was here for a reason, that he had something he must accomplish other than eating, mating, and exploring this Edenic garden, was constantly with him as the precious days trickled on.

Only the others who revealed iridescent flashes of blue when they took to flight spoke in a wordless language that he could understand. Butterflies and moths came in all colors imaginable here, colors he never would have dreamed of seeing with his eyes of the past. He knew from looking at those like himself that the ones who hid brilliance when they folded their wings were a race apart. Only they seemed to tell him more than brief sensations of hunger, thirst, lust, and exhaustion. The coded patterns on their wings flickered frantically, and combined with the rush of myriad emotions, he was able to learn new things. Crucial things.

During the first month, Inácio took some time to acclimate, and to remember. The first thing he realized was that he was not outside. This was a walled garden, hemmed in by transparent doors. He tried to escape when the families with small children visited and pushed one of the doors open, but he was trapped in a corridor between two doors when the one behind him closed. Inevitably, a man he had seen before caught him in a net and returned him to the garden before he could fly to freedom. If he had a mission to accomplish, he would do so among the leaves and vines.

How he could recall certain things, like his daughter's love for the ocean or the basic tenets of his faith, was puzzling enough. How he knew that he only had one hundred fifteen days to live was a mystery. By observing his insect kin, he could deduce that he, too, bore seven rings on each of his wings, rings resembling the iris and pupil of men's eyes. Seven twice over, a number laden with meaning now, just as it had been when he saw from eyes like those.

Nearly every day, people walked through the enclosed tropical forest. Most were fair-skinned, and he knew that this was not where he had come from. In another life, his skin had been caramel brown, and his hair had been dark. He remembered that as the first month came to a close. Names and places fled his patchwork memory, but he knew that much. Spirited to another land, he found himself shying away from the people more often than not, obeying the animal's instinct. But the second month emboldened him, and he began to experiment.

On the forty-second day, he ventured near the twisting, spiraling, impossibly tall structure in the center of the garden. It dazzled him with its vibrant colors, all shades of orange, red, and yellow at once, but it was not a tree. Its branches were perfectly smooth beneath his feet, and they did not have the earthy taste of bark. Light reflected and refracted in its depths, and its cool, hard surface reminded him of the material out of which the transparent doors were crafted. He landed on several branches at varying levels, fluttering higher and higher until his antennae touched the ceiling. Tingling with anticipation, he crawled to the curving tip of a fiery-colored branch and leaped into the air, floating back down to earth in erratic curves and loops.

Despair...Tension...Curiosity? Excitement.

Inácio recognized those emotions. They were what he had felt when he had discovered he was not alone, that the other ones with blue outlined in black on the inside of their wings were like him. He tasted the air, searching for the scent of another butterfly.

There, perched on the edge of the water. A shimmering bolt of color, blinking in and out of sight. Flying toward it and circling just above, he read the patterns on her wings.

She was only three days old and horribly confused. Projecting sympathy to try to calm her, Inácio wished he had hands with which to touch her nonexistent shoulder. Most of the others he had seen were older, and not in such a volatile state. Perhaps there were many like her, and he had just been too distracted by an enticingly rotten fruit or a ray of sunlight to bother paying attention.

Flying in front of her so she could see his wings, he flashed code back at her. *Do you know what to do?* Intangible concepts like purpose and destiny were hard to communicate by way of the wing patterns. But he knew she would understand.

She flickered back at him. *No.*

He fluttered in haphazard circles, accidentally projecting a bit of agitation. She responded to it, still confused.

Do you?

Inácio replied in the negative, having expected that question. All the butterflies he had spoken to were mid-way through their short lives, and just as lost as he was. Blue ones older and wiser than he had to be out there, souls who neared their last days and could die content in the knowledge that they had played their part. He needed to be more vigilant. His eyes perceived so many colors. Sorting through the deluge of visual information that still overwhelmed him, even after a month and a half, would be his first step towards the end.

You will find it. I will, too.

The young female drew her wings closed for a moment, as if pondering what to say next, before she replied with more optimism than before.

You have helped me.

She dipped her head in the pool and drank, then rose into the air and fluttered beyond the range of the wing code. He wondered if he would see her again.

The fifty-sixth day dawned brighter than most before it, and by mid-morning sunlight enveloped the garden in rich, shimmering curtains. Inácio finished his impromptu breakfast in the loam of the forest floor, shook mud from his feet, and was about to continue his never-ending search when he realized that another butterfly lay on the ground, the seven rings of one wing facing upward. He felt sadness first, but quickly realized it was not dead. Not yet, at least. Seizing his chance, he flew over to it, projecting urgency so it would speak to him.

The butterfly fluttered its wings limply, but did not open them. This one was a female as well, but she was approaching her last hours. Flapping in frustration, he moved in front of her so she could see the code.

Wake! Stay alive! I don't know what to do!

The elderly female twitched her antennae, and against all odds, she opened her wings in a slow, laborious movement. He quickly flew around to read the patterns.

My task is done.

Inácio would have screamed had he the voice to. Instead he flew back into her field of view.

But what was it?

She convulsed. *It is not the same as yours. None of us have the same task....*

32

Her wings closed, and a spasm wracked her fragile form every few seconds, but she could not open them again. He could sense her calm resignation, her acceptance of the end that would come very soon. She was not afraid. She had found peace.

Crushed, he left her there, waiting to die. She was of no more use to him.

By the seventieth day, he had nearly given up on ever realizing his unknown dream. Over half of his life was gone, and he was no closer to his goal than when he had crawled from the viscous cage of birth. He had mated with several females, obeying the incessant tug of his nature—one of them had been the butterfly he had met by the water when she was so young. She was just as lacking in answers as he, but had welcomed the distraction from their hunt for something higher. They found each other again as the middle month of life ended, and they knew they were providing second chances for future wandering spirits. But this was not their task; every butterfly procreated. Something unique was waiting for him. If only he could find it before he, too, fell to the ground.

On the ninety-eighth day of one butterfly's life, seven-year-old Caitlyn Kennedy walked into Franklin Park Conservatory, lingering behind the laughing, screeching, running gaggle of children. She always felt a bit better at summer camp, because they went on visits to neat places. Last week they went to COSI, the only science museum in Columbus, and that was a blast. She had almost forgotten that her mother had smacked her arm so hard that it left a bruise the size of a cup coaster. Thankfully, the mark was easily hidden under her sleeve that week. She would have been awfully hot if she had to wear a sweater to cover up anything more obvious.

No one had asked questions this morning when she came to camp with a black eye. She was red-haired, pale, and freckled, so it only stood out more plainly, but everyone had simply nodded when her mother told the counselor with an exasperated smile how she had been at the playground and banged herself on the merry-go-round. Caitlyn could imagine that she had actually enjoyed herself at the playground and become rowdy enough to warrant a black eye that way.

She still trailed behind the others, but jogged to catch up when they entered the first hall of plants. The room was sweltering and uncomfortable, especially with this many children packed closely together, and the tour guide's voice went in one of Caitlyn's ears and out the other. It was not the guide's fault; she was more than enthusiastic, and most of the other campers were excited about the exotic plants with spiky flowers and the vines sprawling over tree trunks, just like in *The Jungle Book*. But she could not fully appreciate any of it. Her eye hurt. She was hot. And she had barely slept the night before. *Hopefully*, she thought, *this trip will be over soon.*

They passed through several rooms, and she perked up a bit in the desert biome, where the air was not so sticky. The guide said one of the plants that almost never bloomed was in flower just for them. The huge rose-shaped succulent with pointed tips on the ends of its leaves was called a century plant, just for that reason—it might bloom only once a century. Its tall, flowering stalk sprouting out of the center was quite a sight. Caitlyn also liked the tree with the thousands of tiny leaves that spread fuzzies all over the rocky sand. It was cute. She started to feel better.

Before they entered the Pacific Island Water Garden, the guide told them that there would be lots of butterflies in the room. She said they could touch them if the insects landed on them, but otherwise should leave them alone. Caitlyn closed her eyes as she walked into the garden, then opened them, just to make it more exciting. She gasped.

Butterflies were everywhere. On the flowers, in the trees, and by a little pool. She recognized the monarchs from school, but all the other ones were new to her. High on a cloud of her own amazement, she drifted away from the group and stopped

34

by the banana tree. There, on a very brown piece of fruit hanging down in a bunch, was a giant, brilliant-blue butterfly. She had never seen one so bright.

Dazed, she reached out to touch it, and it turned around to look at her with its tiny insect eyes. She held her breath. Its antennae swiveled back and forth. She could imagine that it was studying her, just as amazed as she was. After all, she must look like a big monster. Slowly, gradually, she moved her hand towards it again, hoping against hope that it would land on her finger.

Instead, the blue butterfly abruptly flew away, as if something else had caught its attention. Something more important than she was. Crestfallen, Caitlyn walked back to the group, but she was subdued the rest of the time they were in the conservatory. She knew it was only a dumb bug, but somehow she had expected more. That was her life. Expectations never fulfilled.

Later that evening, after all the children were gone, a single blue butterfly that shone like a star tried to escape one more time through the transparent door. One of the familiar men, a tender of the garden, shut the door more quickly than usual behind him. The butterfly's wing tore off in the door, and the insect fell to the floor, writhing before lying still. The next morning it was dead.

Though he recalled nothing of the last time, when the moment for which he was born dissolved into what could have been, Inácio knew his name when he emerged from the chrysalis.

Cynthia Rosi

At the age of 20, Cynthia Rosi emigrated on her own from Seattle to London determined to write for a living. She landed a reporting job with the North London Advertiser series of newspapers, leading to a senior reporting position at the *Hornsey Journal*. She left news to run the PR department at the international moving company Pickfords.

As a reporter in London, Cynthia wrote hundreds of news and feature articles. Credits in the UK included the *Daily Express*, *The Guardian*, *Mountain Biker*, *You*, and *Bella*.

Headline published Rosi's novels *Motherhunt* and *Butterfly Eyes* (now on e-book).

Since moving to Columbus, Ohio, Cynthia has written and produced 20 episodes of *The Conscious Voices* program on WCRS. Her writing credits include *The Christian Science Monitor*, *The Grapevine*, and *Green Woman*. In 2007, she won the Ohio Writer's Contest for her short story "Salmon."

Cynthia Rosi blogs at www.simplyhugyourself.com, and her website is www.cynthiarosi.com.

NEAR MISS
By Cynthia Rosi

I stood outside the Northstar Café, waiting for Ian, feeling leggy in my flip-flops, blue cotton mini-skirt and white halter-neck, letting the afternoon heat swaddle me like a cocoon. That July day had to have been summer's hottest. Trees lining High Street wilted, their dusty green leaves gasping for a thunderstorm, but I loved the way the heat embraced me. In July, my skin seemed to open and suck in the light.

Ian had called me a couple weeks back and asked me out to lunch. I chose the Northstar Café because I could almost afford it, and I could bike there from my apartment two miles away on Greenlawn. That would mean we couldn't ride home together in his Nissan Micra: I didn't want to fall into bed—again—with Ian.

We got a little table toward the back of the restaurant. I had the Buddha bowl; he bought a veggie burger, made a face at it.

"Why'd you buy that?" I asked. "You look like you'd rather eat meat."

"Aren't you a vegetarian?" he asked, watching me stab a forkful of tofu.

"Living with my brother? The halal butcher? Have you seen the contents of our fridge?"

"That's right. George is…" Ian pitched his voice low into a gravely stage whisper, "…the *butcher of Greenlawn*."

My thing with Ian is weird. When he hired me at The Limited a year ago we didn't have any chemistry. I quit six months later to go freelance into design, but kept up with Ian. He's this tall skinny guy with lank black hair and dark brown eyes, and he looks at you like he needs taking care of, but really he's assessing how far he can get, how fast. I don't know why he let me in on that; maybe because he's hot, and I'm not.

Sometimes I let my bra straps show, sometimes I don't shave my pits, sometimes I forget to wear makeup or take off

37

my old nail polish. Ian likes white-blondes, nails-dipped-in-chicken's-blood, black mascara, and a body that could be in a bikini ad.

I've got my attention on other things. I like Columbus art collectives. I like going to galleries and hanging out with the owners. Mainstream guys like Ian usually make me feel like someone is stepping on my chest.

While we talked, I felt for a connection. It's this secret thing I've done since I was a little kid. I try to imagine I'm listening to the person's soul when they talk. I lock my eyes on their face and then I *feel* for how far back they are. I feel for their real voice. Sometimes it's a whisper. Sometimes it's a person who feels desperate. Or dead.

"There's this new manager, Shanti," Ian began.

Oh. So we were back to hot Ian and quirky Jess, talking about his work. *Why does he need me to do this with him?* I wondered.

"They're training her with Tom, that nerdy bean counter. He just sees what's right in front of him. She's interesting, you know? I think she's intelligent, like you…"

I'm sure I was glazed over, but not so meditative that I didn't notice the bone he'd thrown. As he talked, he seemed to recede farther and farther back into his brain, as if he'd become very small and very anxious. It was almost a little kid persona talking to me now. A small, frightened little kid.

Northstar Café gets very busy on a Saturday afternoon, and the line wound outside the door for people wanting to be served, their necks craning for tables. Ian finished his food and got up to go. I half-stood, and kissed him on the cheek.

"I always feel better after talking with you, Jess," he said.

"You know it's rude to talk about other women, don't you Ian? I'm going to get sick of it," I told him.

"I'll make it up to you," he said.

Not in bed, I promised myself. "You can take me out dancing, or to Shadowbox. I like Shadowbox."

38

As I sat down, I knew Ian would call me with tickets, and then he'd want to sleep with me. I sat staring into the kernels of brown rice at the bottom of my Buddha bowl, moving them around with a cube of tofu speared on my fork. All men were like Ian. Except George. Even my own dad had womanized behind Mom's back. I used to think he was God. Both my parents lived with someone different now.

"Is anybody sitting here?"

It's rare that a stranger asks to sit at your table, especially one who looks interesting. But this guy was about twenty-four and all blue eyes, with a soft mop of dark hair cut up over his ears but left longish on top. I noticed his fingers—square at the tips. They reminded me of antennae. The OSU jersey and the Levis screamed at me.

"My friend left," I said. "I'm nearly done."

I ate the rest of the scraps in my Buddha bowl slowly, past the point of fullness, wondering if I should start talking to this guy. We did the shared table thing of looking away from each other. He went to the restroom and asked me to hold his seat, and then I went to the restroom while he saved mine for me.

By the time I got back they'd cleared the table, and there was coffee and cake sitting at my place. My hackles went up. Some table-mate! I was just about to say "Thanks for saving my spot," with my best sneer, when he said: "They've got these terrific brownies here and I ordered one but I got burned out on them last week, so would you like mine? I got coffee to go with it."

My face cracked open with a wide, surprised smile. "I love their brownies but I'm on a budget, so I only get them once a month," I babbled. "Thanks!"

He introduced himself as Jared. He'd graduated in architecture two years ago, but because of the economy was still taking short-term contracts.

"I know what that's like," I nodded, cutting into a brownie with the side of my fork. "I graduated from CCAD the same time as you. I get work on and off, mostly web design. But I make costumes for theater productions at night." I scooped up the brownie. "Things can get pretty tight between jobs," I finished, and popped the bite into my mouth.

Even though I knew I'd have to do some serious tummy-sucking-in when I got up from the table if I wasn't going to look like I'd gained five pounds, I ate the entire brownie and drank the coffee to the bottom of the cup. I wanted to draw it out with Jared. He got me talking about living on Greenlawn, and what did I think about neighborhood gentrification and the property slowdown.

"Have you been to that new winery on Front Street?" he asked. "They've got live music and a glass artist installation."

That would have been the time to look hard at him, to really try to see the brain cogs that drove his body, but I felt so excited about a date with a guy who didn't talk about other women that the words "yes" and "what time?" fell out of my mouth.

I had a terrible week. The microwave blew up breakfast. I mean literally blew up—a spark and a BANG, and my burrito was still half frozen. George called the landlord, but the electrician he sent did something to the Internet. We were without service for the next three days, while Time Warner argued with the landlord about who killed the connection.

The time slipped away from me, and all of a sudden it was Thursday afternoon. *Jared, at the winery, 7:30 Friday night. What am I going to wear?* I drove to Rag-O-Rama, then the Goodwill, not in town but out to Powell. I ended up with a tight-fitting black sateen mini-skirt with a side zip and pleats, and a fuchsia silk shirt. I ripped the buttons off the shirt and sewed on these funky fruit buttons and fitted the waist. Then, I carefully sheared off the sleeves, cut them into strips, and braided the strips into a loose belt.

I got to the winery at 7:35. Jared told me it was across the street from a firm of architects he'd been courting. We perched

40

on stools at oak-barrel tables and drank wine with our antipasto and salad. He wore a black V-neck t-shirt that revealed his biceps, and Levi's with black Converses that made me think of quick getaways.

As we sat together sipping, he grabbed a pen and began to draw the building, sketching fast in very straight lines which he went over and over for emphasis, until some were ruts in the napkin, carving it up with his pen as he described arches and sub-basements.

"My father's a judge—he took me down into the corridors that link the buildings," he explained. I stared at his chin and for a moment I fell into him. It felt like a building under construction, steel girders and perpendicular angles going up and down, square structures like a high-rise before its floors are poured and the windows fitted, like the struts of a cube. It felt extremely solid, and airy, and it scared me.

The Jared I saw would make me practice my art for 2.15 hours every day before we went for a half hour walk, and feed me precisely six rolls of sushi for lunch, because he'd calculated out the protein optimal for my height and body fat.

"There's a passage that goes to the river," he continued. "They think the Underground Railroad…Jess?"

I shook my head. "I went all foggy for a second."

"I could see that." He put down his pen, picked up his glass.

I'd ticked him off. "It's a lot to take in. The building, the history…"

"The wine," he conceded.

I folded the napkin and tucked it into a jacket pocket. "A souvenir."

He leaned forward and kissed me. I'd wanted to kiss him since the Northstar Café. As I enjoyed the warmth, the brush of his lips, the clean smell of his skin, I also felt a resistance inside myself.

When we'd pulled back and picked up our wine glasses, I

asked: "So, your dad's a judge? What's that like?"

Jared frowned. "Let's just say that OSU and architecture wasn't my parents' plan. Dad had me down for law at Yale."

"Ouch."

"I hate law. It's not justice. People get processed through a system. The people who dole out the punishments get trapped. They don't escape it. You really live on Greenlawn? Do you know how many people die there every year?"

"I feel safe. I live with my brother."

He stared at his hands. Then he looked up. "Did you know this place used to be a speak-easy during Prohibition?"

We walked over to the Outland. I hated how loud it was, but I loved moving my body to that industrial music. I shook myself loose from all those serious feelings I'd had over dinner. Jared moved fluidly, dancing himself into a frenzy next to me, but staying close, keeping eye contact a lot. At two a.m. he followed me back to Greenlawn in his Jetta. He kept checking over his shoulder as he walked me through the parking lot and all the way up the flight of steps and onto my landing.

"Who's that?" I backed into Jared.

"Is that your apartment?"

We'd both stopped, staring at the man passed out against the door in a crouch, posed like those 1950s pictures of Mexicans in sombreros snoozing underneath a tree, his face in his arms hugged around his knees.

I began to slowly tug Jared forward. "It's Ian."

I relaxed. Jared didn't. "Who's Ian?" he said.

"This guy I knew when I worked for The Limited. I wonder why he's here."

I leaned past Ian and put my key into the metal gate's lock. As I shoved the gate open, Ian fell against the door. I unlocked the door and with a little hop I was inside.

"Are you just going to leave him there?" Jared wondered aloud, in a don't-wake-the-baby tone of voice.

"I don't know what to do," I whispered back. "He'll get

robbed, if he hasn't already had his pockets picked." I thought of George's charts.

George and I used to play this game, "How Low Does it Go?" We'd leave stuff around to see if it would get swiped. Once I put a gumball ring next to an empty Coke on the roof of my car. Someone swiped the ring. We tried underpants, a coffee mug, half of a cigarette. George would time how long until the item was gone.

I only agreed to the apartment because my brother is as solid as the side of a brick building, and he didn't mind always walking me to my car. We could hear gunshots from the crack house two blocks north at three a.m., and from the ghetto nightclub, too. George carried a tiny gun in his pocket. I was always afraid he'd forget the safety and shoot off his balls.

Jared stepped around Ian and grabbed him under the armpits. "Phew. How much did he drink?"

Jared dragged Ian through the doorjamb, Ian's legs stretching as his body swept the green linoleum floor.

"I only know him from work. We've been to lunch a couple times." I dissembled. "He's usually talking about his dates. He's always got a string of women."

"Looks like he got dumped." Jared laid Ian on the floor and closed the door. I balled up a tea towel and stuck it under Ian's head.

"Should we check him for exit wounds? Or see that he's breathing?" I suggested.

Jared crouched, got to all fours and put his ear to Ian's mouth. "He stinks. And he's breathing." He opened Ian's brown leather jacket. "No blood."

Jared rolled Ian into the recovery position, and stood up. We looked at Ian together, like staring at a smushed animal.

I could feel that Jared wanted to go. Evenings like ours were supposed to end on the couch, or at least with both of us agreeing we'd go out again but both of us knowing that we wouldn't. Thing was, I'd wanted our evening to end on the couch. But now my shitty week seemed to be concluding with the irritating date dynamic of Jared wanting to escape.

"Look," I said, keeping my voice down to not wake George. "I didn't ask for this. This week I got my car towed and the landlord screwed up the electricity, and now I've got an unconscious former colleague about to puke all over my floor. *I* wanted to have coffee with you. *I* actually wanted to see you again."

Jared raised his eyebrows.

"You make the coffee," he suggested. "I'll try to wake him up. Maybe we can put him in a cab."

"Thank you," I said, and slipped my arms around Jared's waist and hugged him. We stood like that for a moment, snuggling, the energy building between our bodies.

"Do you have any ice?" asked Jared. "Or frozen peas?"

I found a bag of frozen corn and filled a tumbler with ice, and Jared crouched beside Ian and put the frozen corn against his face.

I began to make a pot of coffee, keeping an eye on Jared and Ian. I really didn't want Ian vomiting on my floor.

"Ian, wake up! You need to wake up now. Ian!" Jared called, and then unbuttoned the top of Ian's shirt and put a handful of ice cubes onto his chest.

"Oh shit," Ian mumbled. "Shit!" He backed up and reached into his shirt and fumbled for the ice. "What the fuck!"

Jared stood up and handed me the bag of corn. "Job done."

"Ian, what are you doing here?" I demanded. I was frightened, because I knew what he wanted.

"I was in the neighborhood," he said. "Where've you been?"

"On a date. Don't look so surprised," I spat. I was angry at Ian for thinking I'd help him, that he could drop in completely wasted. I could see myself in a new mirror, as if Jared held it up. *I'd* been keeping Ian sniffing around, because I wanted a fail-safe, a back-pocket "just in case." I wasn't any better than

44

Ian. I'd created half of this mess, and it couldn't have plopped into my lap at a worse time.

"We'll call you a cab," Jared said.

Ian looked from Jared to me. "Sure. Where's the bathroom?"

"Straight down the hall. The door on the left," I told him.

The kitchen smelled of coffee perking. I took milk out of the fridge and handed mugs to Jared. "Could you warm up the milk?" I asked him. "I better check on him."

I turned into the hall, but something was wrong. The door to George's room was ajar.

"Ian!" I called out, "That's not the bathroom! Don't go in there!"

"Put that back, you idiot!" George roared.

I raced down the hallway. Half asleep, Ian held his penis in his hand, as if he were about to pee on George's bed. George held his tiny gun out, pointed at Ian.

"George! He's wasted. I sent him to the bathroom. Put that gun down!"

Jared raced down the hall. "What's going on?"

Suddenly, there was an almighty BANG. The apartment fell into total darkness. "He shot me!" Ian wailed. "He shot me! Call an ambulance!"

I could see George in an orange jumpsuit. Mom and Dad, sitting a chilly distance away from each other in a courtroom pew, staring daggers at me. And Jared, the judge's son, standing in the witness box, looking down on us all.

"I did not!" George protested. "What happened to my light? Why won't my light go on?"

Jared took out his cell phone and George flipped his own open, and they glared at each other in a greenish light.

George threw the little gun on the bed. "If I'd really wanted to kill him, I would have grabbed one of my knives." He gestured toward a roll of knives he kept on his nightstand, sharpened for work.

"There's nothing wrong with you," George told Ian, who was stuffing himself back into his pants.

"Then what was that noise?" Ian complained, sobering up.

George and I looked at each other.

"The microwave?" I offered.

"I plugged it in," said Jared, "to heat up the milk."

Ian wanted to walk home, but George insisted on taking him in the car. I know George felt bad about scaring Ian, and I wondered how close he'd come to pulling that trigger. What if Ian *had* peed on George? Those are the parts of life that you lock away and never examine.

Jared and I sat on the sofa and stared at the candles we'd put on the coffee table. I had too much adrenaline pumping through my bloodstream to need coffee, so I'd put my mug down. Jared seemed to be considering his.

"I'm sorry," I apologized. "I really am."

"You didn't do anything," said Jared.

"Would you ever go out with me again?" I asked.

My question hung in the air. Jared didn't answer. After a moment he said: "It is very interesting at your house."

"It's not always like this," I said. "Mostly my brother goes to work, and I work on my designs. It's actually really quiet around here."

"He's the butcher?"

I nodded. "Halal. He can really rant on about it. We'll never run out of meat. If you like goat."

He put his coffee down on the table, and half stood up. I leaned forward and put my face in my hands. Maybe it would be best this way. Jared would need a Yale girl for his father's Christmas parties.

I tried to keep my shoulders from shaking. I crammed my hand in my skirt pocket for a tissue and came up with Jared's napkin.

"I should go," he said. I trailed him to the door. He gave

me a goodbye kiss chaste enough for a grandma.

I sunk back down on the sofa, pulled a pillow into my chest, and stared into the room. I love July nights, for their warmth, their close blanket of heat, but tonight I didn't revel in the darkness. When George came back he left me sitting.

I fell asleep with my arms wrapped around the pillow, and the sun came up.

At ten a.m. I'm dealing with the electrician again, my hair pulled back in a scrunchy, in my sweats trying to get the electricity fixed so I can shower. The electrician's going in and out with his box, and I'm cleaning cupboards so I have something to do in the kitchen while I babysit the door so people don't wander through.

I hear a knock and shout "Come in!" to the electrician while I wipe the sponge around the baseboards. Someone's standing behind me. In the corner of my vision, I see a cardboard box. I stand up quickly, grabbing the counter's edge to steady myself, and come face to face with Jared.

"Doughnuts?" he offers.

I'm thinking how I must smell, and that I haven't showered, and…

He looks me over. "It's really interesting at your house," he says, quietly. Then he smiles, extends the box and asks, "Do you want to eat these on the sofa?"

William J. Hallal

William J. Hallal was born and raised in Cleveland, Ohio. He attended Catholic schools for thirteen years before his father's die-hard football fandom pushed him towards The Ohio State University. In 2011, he graduated with a B.A. in English and a Minor in Creative Writing, after completing a senior thesis, a novella and four short stories under the guidance of Lee K. Abbott, head of the school's Creative Writing Department.

Today, William lives in the Short North and works as a tutor for student athletes at OSU's Younkin Success Center.

The idea for "Suicide Guys" came during a bout of homesickness and frustration during the author's study abroad at the University of Greenwich in London. He had been working on several pieces with a snarky and irreverent narrator, but it was only after reading *Tunneling to the Center of the Earth*, Kevin Wilson's seminal debut story collection, that the author had the idea to write a story about a job too strange to be real.

"Suicide Guys" initially had a much bleaker tone, but a workshop with OSU professor Erin McGraw helped bring humor and character to the story. The narrator is not based on the author, but they do share similar concerns and face similar issues: religion, guilt, and growing up.

Please visit SelfTerminate.com for objective advice.

SUICIDE GUYS
By William J. Hallal

It's a frigid Tuesday morning in Columbus when I arrive at the office of SelfTerminate.com. Even for Ohio, the snow is severe, and I have to shake off an accumulation of inches from my pea coat and boots before I step in. This is school-canceling snow, the kind I would have cheered for when I was growing up on the east side of Cleveland so I could stay in and play computer games. As I step through the door of our Short North office, I think of the hundreds of hours I logged on that basement computer in my old house. Had I been a more outdoors kind of kid, I wonder if I would have grown up to create a website for suicide.

Daryl Kaminski, the site's web designer and co-founder, has beaten me to work yet again. "Daryl," I say, uncharacteristically upbeat for this time of year. "My main man. How the hell are you?"

"Okay," he says, and swerves his chair back towards his monitor. Daryl and I are friends of several years and former roommates, but when it comes to social graces, he's a step or two removed from Dustin Hoffman in *Rain Man*. I went through four years of high school without saying a word to the kid, and I might have gone another four in college had I not needed a man with technical know-how to back my insane website idea.

"Got an e-mail from Nora Wilmington last night," I say. Most co-workers would comment on the weather, but Daryl has no instinct for small talk. Mention the Internet and he's all ears. Our common bond is the Internet. It entered the mainstream around the time we entered puberty, and as it developed its offbeat, cynical, and at times messed-up sense of humor, so did we.

"Do I know her?" he asks. Daryl can spit out lines upon lines of complex computer code, but remembering the people who cause him discomfort is a Herculean feat.

"She was in our class at Mayfield," I tell him. "Chubby girl, very upbeat, very perky." Another trait Daryl and I share is our disdain for the chronically happy. I suppose if either of us were similarly afflicted, we wouldn't have started a website with "terminate" in the title. Another memory of Nora finds me, this one oddly relevant. "She was the head of the suicide prevention program at school. She used to hand out prevention pamphlets." I let out a laugh, not a nice one. "At first I thought she wanted to use the site."

Daryl gives an odd sort of grunt, not quite laughter but not quite disapproval. Maybe it's sympathy. In retrospect, Nora's giddy disposition probably covered up a profound sadness, not unlike the one I suspect Daryl heaps upon himself for no other reason than being Catholic and feeling guilty all the time.

"Anyway," I say, "she wants to organize a class reunion. Think we should go?"

Daryl visibly shudders at the thought of returning to high school. "I don't think so," he says.

"Seven-year reunion," I say. "Strange number." But when I think about it, twenty-five is a strange age. At earlier high school reunions and those drunken college Thanksgivings, we were filled with anticipation of the legal drinking age and a bachelor's degree. Now, we have nothing to look forward to but lower car insurance rates. And marriage and kids, if you're into that sort of thing.

"Did she say anything else?" Daryl asks. I shake my head. Scrolling through my inbox, I can see there are some threatening e-mails from the Foundation for Friendly Families—FoFerFa, as Daryl and I like to call them—and I find myself hoping Daryl didn't get them. Their allegations are predictable: that we glorify suicide, erode the common morality. Not everyone understands the humor in what we're doing. These emails have never bothered me, but I think they get to Daryl's religious side. My stance on them is Carroll Draper Problem-Solving Method #1: If we make fun of it, it will eventually go away.

"I might've gone to the reunion if it was last month," I

say, smiling ruefully. "I could have shown off Gwen to those assholes." Gwen and I dated for about five-and-a-half months, breaking it off a few weeks ago just before the crucial half-year mark. I suspected it wouldn't last. She looked down on my movie poster collection, resented my general lack of organization, and seemed to think eating out should entail more than Chinese food.

"Who's Gwen?" asks Daryl.

"My ex-girlfriend," I tell him. "You knew that, Daryl."

"Oh," he says. "I don't think I met her."

"I'm sure I introduced you." I realize as I say it that I didn't arrange a meeting for Gwen and Daryl, I never even tried. With Daryl, sometimes it doesn't seem worth trying. I'm able to coax him into conversation by myself, but around women he clams up completely. I used to try to play wing-man for him at bars, but sometime before graduation I gave up on fixing him up with anyone. I once joked with him that he should become a priest, but he didn't laugh. I haven't brought it up since.

"Did she dump you?" Daryl's bluntness, after all these years, can still be surprising. The truth is that though there have been five relationships of a similar length in my tumultuous post-college years (with a slight overlap on two of them), I have cared for them all more than I admitted, and Gwen's leave-taking still smarts. One of Gwen's reasons for leaving me was that I lived and behaved, generally, "like a goddamn child." Yet I also seem to remember her saying something about me being too dedicated to my work.

But, if we're being honest here, she may also have mentioned having a strong moral opposition to what I do for a living. That's a common reaction among women I've dated. You can only tell them you work as an "online consultant" for so long before they start asking questions.

Daryl interrupts my reverie to tell me he's having trouble with a user's survey. "He's not giving me anything to work with," he says.

"They always give you something to work with," I

say. I think back to the early days of the site, when people's constraints merely encouraged our creativity. We'd just graduated from college, had just started to make money off the site, and the suggestions were wild. There was the guitar player in New Mexico we instructed to wander into a wolves' den wearing a suit made entirely of raw meat. There was the unemployed investment banker in New York we encouraged to stand under the Empire State building and have someone drop a penny on his head. My favorite was the octogenarian with the username "Big Frank" who we recommended to commit suicide by orgy.

Daryl shakes his head. "He hates guns. He's afraid of needles. He doesn't live within fifty miles of a skyscraper or a tall building. I'm thinking about just telling him we can't help him."

"Where does he live?" I ask.

"The Upper Peninsula of Michigan," he says.

"Easy fix," I say. "Drowning. He's surrounded by lakes." I shake my head even as I mention it—we really have lost our creative streak.

"He's afraid of water."

"Damn," I say. "How old is this guy?"

"Uh…he's twelve."

"No way." I wheel my chair over to Daryl's desk and check the survey. "When I was twelve, I had to get permission from my mom to visit the Nickelodeon website. And it took five hours to load with dial-up. Kids today have everything."

"Aren't you concerned about this?" he asks.

"Well, Daryl," I say, assuming my corporate tone. "Since the site is not intended for actual use, I see no reason to enforce any age restriction."

"But he's so young," Daryl says.

"I agree. That is one messed-up twelve-year-old."

"Aren't you worried about the ethics?"

"The great thing about this site is that no one takes it as seriously as you and I do." I pat him on the shoulder. The pat is a little awkward, since Daryl is allergic to all forms of physical contact. "Tell you what. If it will ease your mind, I'll handle his survey for you."

"You sure?" he asks.

"I love a challenge," I say.

"I'll send it to you right away," he says.

"Thanks." I wheel back to my desk. "But really, the kid lives in northern Michigan. How could he *not* want to kill himself?" Daryl does not laugh, and I turn my chair back to my computer.

Daryl was right. This twelve-year-old is not going to make his suicide easy.

Today is a rare day I've taken work home, to a one-bedroom in Italian Village. It has been cluttered, to say the least, since Gwen left, and though she never moved in I still find artifacts of her visits: yesterday, a toothbrush under the sink; today, a bran cereal I'd never eat. *Young*, I think. *Everyone in this city is so young.* I toss the box into the trash.

There are plenty of families and old folks out in the suburbs, but stay long enough in my neighborhood and you'll be shocked by the sight of a non-homeless man over forty. Gwen was twenty-two, barely out of college. The kids who skateboard in the park across the street, the hipster couples holding hands, the jersey-clad frat boys making their way to the Arena District—young. All that youth is fun at first, and exciting, but after a while it gets exhausting.

And now this twelve-year-old. This kid has a strangely developed sense of gallows humor, but he's afraid of anything remotely death-related. No guns and no needles. He refuses to work with rope as well (bad P.E. accident, he claims). I can't recommend that he leave his car running in the garage, for obvious reasons. And when I try to get creative, I have to worry: do pre-teens understand sarcasm? If I tell him to go to downtown Detroit and hold up a racist sign, like Bruce Willis in *Die Hard 3*, will he actually do it? Has he even *seen* that movie?

The window on our twenty-four-hour suicide recommendation guarantee is running out, so I write a hasty but professional-sounding email explaining that the site is experiencing technical difficulties and his information was lost. It will buy us some time.

I've barely walked through the office door the next day when Daryl asks me about the twelve-year-old. "I told him there was a server crash," I say.

Daryl looks relieved. "Good," he says. "Hopefully he won't re-submit."

"Are you kidding?" I say. "I can't wait for him to send another one in. No way that kid is gonna stump me."

"Oh." Daryl turns back to his desk and says nothing for over an hour. Not an entirely uncommon occurrence, as light conversation never comes easily to Daryl, but the silence has a slight heft to it. It is possible, I suppose, that this user is troubling Daryl more than he's letting on. But before I can think of a way to ask him, a message pops up in my inbox from a woman named Olivia Bendrix. The name doesn't sound familiar, but the subject line is "Mr. Carroll Draper." I open it and read.

'To Mr. Carroll Draper. We have never met, but my husband was a user on your website.' What jumps out at me immediately is the use of past tense in connection with her husband. Divorce? I read on: 'I am currently living in Columbus, and I would like to meet you at the Northstar Café on High Street.' She gives a time for tomorrow morning, a dash, and her name.

"Daryl," I say, then realize that whatever it is I'm going to find out, he doesn't have to know. Despite his apparent lack of emotion, Daryl can be a sensitive guy. I don't want to upset him over nothing. And if it's not nothing? Well, better to leave him out entirely for now. "If I gave you ten bucks, could you run across the street and get us some sandwiches?" Another nice thing about Daryl—he'll never complain about getting anything for you. Must be some kind of Catholic thing.

I wait for Daryl to leave the room, then I type my response to Olivia Bendrix. But before I do—and I hate myself a little, even while I'm doing it—I type her name into Google and see what comes up in images.

At the café I order coffee and sit down. I'm almost half an hour early, so I figure I'll have time to read the paper before she gets here. I'm wrong. As soon as I look up there's a strange woman sitting at my table cradling a glass of orange juice like a tumbler of whiskey.

"Are you Carroll Draper?" she asks.

Olivia Bendrix does not look quite like her Google result. In the picture online, she was model-gorgeous—why did you think I decided to go? In person, she's older than I expected. Her looks and style of dress say she can't be more than four years older than me, yet she lacks the twenty-something stench of desperation and diminishing career options. Her calm poise and slightly heavy amount of eye make-up place her in her early thirties. She's well-dressed, mostly in black. Her eyes are brown and piercing. If you were to look across a bar and raise your eyebrows in her direction, you'd look down fast the moment she turned those eyes on you. That's how I felt the moment she sat down—guilty, like I had been ogling her and she had come to my table specifically to tell me off.

"Yes," I say. "And you are Mrs. Bendrix? Or is it Ms. Bendrix?"

"Olivia is fine," she says curtly. She isn't rude, exactly, but it's clear she is a woman with a purpose. Without knowing why, a panic begins to rise in my throat. I do my best to stay collected.

"Right. Olivia. So…"

"I came to thank you."

This is not what I expected to hear. "Why?" I ask.

Olivia examines the pulp in her glass. "I've been going

through my husband's things for a month now. Last night I got to his laptop. I went through his history and I found your site."

"Your husband," I begin. "Is he…?"

"He died last month," she says.

I clear my throat, uncomfortable and also terrified. "How did he die?"

Olivia stirs the ice in her drink. "He was admitted to the E.R. at Riverside with a broken ankle. He stole two I.V.s of morphine and overdosed. Died in his sleep." She looks up. "My husband had chronic pain," she explains. "Not the aches and pains of aging. Severe pain in his entire body. It started in his stomach, then made its way upward. Then downward. The doctors couldn't stop it. He was on seven different pain meds with no effect. He was chewing them like candy towards the end."

I cross my legs and shift in my seat. Chronic pain had come up as a pre-existing condition in one of my surveys, couldn't have been more than a few months ago. The user name had something to do with jazz.

"I found out he had visited your site five times in the past two months. He got some fairly obvious suggestions. Leave the car running in the garage. Mix pain meds to cause liver failure. Use his father's service pistol." She shudders. "But the last one suggested morphine. It was a complicated plan, but it was laid out in great detail. Painless, as far as death goes. I think it appealed to his sense of irony." She almost smiles. "Was it you?"

I am faced with the dilemma of trying to remember something while simultaneously making an effort to block it out completely. I couldn't have been responsible. Daryl and I, we didn't have anything to do with the death of some stranger who happened to live in Columbus. And yet, here's the proof. Here's the widow.

"See, our site," I manage to say, "has this privacy policy. There are a number of, ah, concerns—"

"Did you think I came here to scream at you?" she asks.

She's got me there. "I don't know why you came," I say.
"Would you have apologized?"

I have to be careful with what I say. All kinds of
responsibility, moral and legal, hovers inches above my head. I
try to use the corporate tone. "My site," I say, "is not intended
for actual use."

"I read the fine print," she said. "My husband was in pain,
and you helped him. I wanted to thank you." She stood up and
grabbed her purse and jacket. "But if you can't take blame, you
can't accept thanks, can you?"

I want to answer her, but all that pops into my head is
Clyde Murvis. I keep thinking over and over again, Clyde
Murvis, Clyde Murvis. Back at Mayfield, Clyde had the idea
to grease the freshman hallway with Crisco and K.Y., which
was hilarious until our librarian, Mrs. Curtis, slipped and broke
her arm. That's how I feel sitting at this table with this woman:
caught in high school, blamed for a prank gone wrong. There's
always a Mrs. Curtis who ruins it for everyone.

"Olivia, you'll have to excuse me," I say. "I just never
thought I would be in this position."

"What position is that?" she asks.

"I never thought anyone would actually, you know, use the
site."

"I never thought I'd be a widow before forty." Olivia
shrugs. "Life's full of surprises."

This could be bad for the site.

That night I try to watch the ten o'clock news, but I can't
stop imposing myself over the headlines. "OSU Alum Assists
Online Euthanasia." Local reporters read grimly to the camera
over footage of me being dragged from my apartment by police.
I turn off the T.V. and start drinking—Carroll Draper Problem-
Solving Method #2. Which is probably how I end up calling
Olivia Bendrix at eleven at night.

"Hello?" She sounds groggy. Shit. I woke her up.

"I'm sorry," I say. "Did I wake you?" I'm remembering

now how every communication breakthrough of my lifetime—instant messaging, texting, Facebook—was made to spare my generation the excruciating pain of the phone call.

"No," she says, her voice distant. "I was just…watching a movie." I'd know that syntax anywhere: the Drunk Girl Slur. She's just as hammered as I am. Of course, she has much more of a right to be.

"What can I do for you?" she asks.

This much I know: I did not put a needle into that man's arm. Feeling bad for something I didn't do is for the God-fearing; Daryl's crowd. Yet: guilt. It's racked my stomach so much I had to toss my barely-touched General Tso's down the garbage disposal. I thought that guilt might be susceptible to beer. That worked for a little while, but right around Beer Four an image came to me of her alone in some Upper Arlington mansion. Olivia, so sad and wise. The youngest widow I know. The only woman I've talked to in any meaningful way since Gwen. I was not kind to her at the café. Thus when Beer Six was done, I looked up Olivia's number from her email and before I could talk myself out of it, began a patented Carroll Draper maneuver: the Grand Drunk Gesture.

"Nothing," I say. Then, quickly: "I'd like to see you." Oh God. I'm supposed to be apologizing. That was the plan. But my throat gets all blocked up at the very thought of it. So what the hell am I doing? Still making a Grand Gesture. Still drunk.

"What about?" she says.

I could be accused of doing some pretty depraved things in my life, but asking a recent widow out on a date would certainly land the lowest on the list. I hesitate, then make the classic follow-up to the Grand Drunk Gesture: the Abrupt About-Face. "Your husband," I say. By nature, the Abrupt About-Face requires some pretty unlikely excuses: "I'm, well, concerned that other users could follow in his steps, and I'd like to get some information about him so we can, ah…"

"You'd like to talk about my husband?" she says. It seems that's all she heard.

I tell her yes. "Meet at Northstar again? Eight o'clock?"

"Better make it noon," she says, and hangs up.

This time I wait at a table for Olivia. She comes in almost twenty minutes late, no make-up this time, bearing all the signs of an afternoon hangover. I ask her how she's doing, and she looks at me carefully.

"Do you really want to know?" she asks. I nod cautiously. "People ask, you see, but they don't want to hear what it's really like. Losing somebody." She stares at the table, then looks up at me. "Have you ever lost someone?"

I shake my head. "What is it like?"

"It's remarkable," she says. "I sit in front of the T.V. for hours without watching a thing. I read entire books without knowing what they're about. I sleep a lot, sometimes most of the day. I don't do a lot of housework. There's a week's worth of dirty laundry on my floor."

It sounds a lot like my apartment. Olivia and I may have more in common than I realized.

"Is there anyone you can talk to?" I ask.

"Our friends are all in New York," she says, "everyone that knew him. His family is out here. It's why we moved. So he could be with them."

"Could you talk to his family?" I ask.

"Please. They're convinced he's in hell."

"Oh," I say.

She crosses her arms. "Those idiots. He was in hell already."

We put in our drink orders at the counter, and upon returning to the table I find myself at a loss for conversation topics. "Religion can be hard on people," I offer, not sure where to go from there. "My partner is a Catholic."

"Your partner?"

"For the website," I explain.

"Is he okay with what you do?"

"I think so. He seems to have reconciled it with his faith."

"Hell of a thing to reconcile," she says.

We order our food and watch the snow fall outside for a moment. "I'm leaving," she says abruptly, "at the end of the month."

"Are you going back to New York?" I ask.

She shakes her head. "New York reminds me too much of him," she says. "And so does here."

"What are you going to do?"

"I'm going to pack up my car and head west," she says. "And see what happens."

We're both quiet for a minute. "Now," I say, removing a folder and a notebook from my knapsack. "I'd like to ask a few questions about your husband."

"I guess we should start with his name," says Olivia.

"Actually," I say, "due to our policy on user privacy, I must ask you not to use his name."

"What are you talking about?"

"It might be easiest if you were to refer to him by his user name, which was...let me check my notes...'ColtraneFan95'."

"That's absurd," she says. "Just let me use his real name."

"Mrs. Bendrix, I have to insist."

"No." People are turning to stare at us. "I want to tell you his name."

"I'm sorry, Olivia," I say.

Olivia gets up without saying a word. She storms into the parking lot and for a moment I am thankful that there are no waitresses in this restaurant, no one to come by and check on my embarrassing progress, no one to let me know that the check will be ready whenever I am.

The twelve-year-old has returned.

It occurs to me, as I sit at home re-reading his survey, that all the wrong people commit suicide. I don't care how high their hormone levels are—people under twenty should be the last ones to commit suicide. There's no way you've fucked up your entire life that young. If kids were to ask me for help (which, thank God, they don't), I would tell them to wait until they're fifty. If by that time, I'd tell them, you still are unable to make connections with people, and there really is no one who loves you in the world, then by all means kill yourself.

But that's the problem. People get too old for suicide. You hardly ever hear about deadbeat dads or retired mass murderers offing themselves. Maybe they should do it more often.

Twelve years old. Jesus Christ.

I get a call from Olivia early the next morning.

"I'm sorry for yelling at you in the restaurant," she says. She clears her throat. "I know you have your reasons for not wanting to know my husband's name. Maybe they're business-related, maybe they're not. Either way, I would like the chance to discuss my husband's life, and his death, if you want. For your research."

"I'd like that very much," I say.

Another pause. "I've been living in cities my whole life," she says, "but I've barely been here eight months. Is there a place you go to get away? When you're, you know, upset?"

"Sometimes I go to the Topiary Garden downtown," I say.

"I'd like to go there," she says.

Problem is, I'm a liar. It's not that I've never been to the Topiary Garden. I've gone plenty of times. Just never when I was upset. In fact, before I met Olivia, I can't remember being this upset about anything.

I try to play it cool when I arrive at work. Daryl and I have lunch in the office. He orders a sub from across the street— turkey and mayo, no lettuce, no cheese. I can't remember the last time I saw him try another sub. I'm tucking into No. 1 Chinese Restaurant's sesame chicken, attacking white rice with my chopsticks and coming up with hardly any.

"What are you doing after work tonight?" Daryl asks.

I look up from my rice. Daryl never asks me that. "Why do you ask?"

"You're wearing cologne and you combed your hair, which you don't normally do for work. You're wearing one of your nicer shirts. I assumed you were dating a new girl or meeting a new one."

Sometimes Daryl seems not to notice you're there, then, like some supercomputer, he'll spit so much information back at you you're amazed he had the storage space for it.

I never get to brag to Daryl, my only co-worker, about my dealings with women. Now the one time he asks, I have to lie. "You got me," I say. "I am going to see a girl."

"Where did you meet her?" asks Daryl.

"The Internet." I don't have to lie entirely.

"Well," he says, "I was wondering if, you know, you wanted to grab a beer or something."

I smile through a mouthful of sesame seeds. "Since when do you invite people out?"

Daryl shrugs. He seems disappointed. "Just thought I'd ask."

"Maybe some other time," I say. But Daryl is already hunched over the sandwich at his desk, and his mouth is full, and he doesn't say anything.

I leave the notebook and folder at home this time. Since Olivia (politely) refused my offer to pick her up, we agreed to meet at the garden entrance at 5:30. I'm late and she's later, so we don't walk through the gate until six. The sun is almost gone and there are no lights in the park. We can barely see the damn topiaries.

The main attraction of the garden is a display of shrubs cut to look like figures from "A Sunny Afternoon on the Isle of La Grande Jatte." I know this not because I am a great lover of art, but because in high school, *Ferris Bueller's Day Off* was my favorite movie. Wise-cracking Ferris, who effortlessly exuded the who-gives-a-shit attitude I tried desperately to imitate, was my idol. It's amazing how long we can pursue our adolescent heroes, even after we've stopped believing in them.

Olivia is quiet as we walk around the park, and I risk teasing her. "Just like Central Park, right?"

"So you've never been to New York, then." Her tone is dry but there might be some slight upward lift to the corners of that slim, wonderfully soft-looking mouth.

"No," I say. "Someday, though."

"You've lived here your whole life?" she asks. I detect incredulity, perhaps pity.

"Born and raised in Cleveland," I say.

"Is that why you're so preoccupied with suicide?"

"Watch enough Browns games and you'd be, too."

Olivia laughs for the first time since I've known her—a quick one, almost bitter-sounding. We pass what might be the famous shrubbery couple with the umbrella. Snow has started falling on the heads of the topiaries, but we keep walking in circles inside the park.

"So how did you first meet your husband?" I ask.

"He was my teacher at NYU," she says. "But it wasn't like that. We didn't date until the end of the semester."

"His survey said he was thirty-eight when he, uh, passed. Is that right?"

"Yes. He was a grad student when we met. He taught me music theory."

"You two were musicians?"

Olivia shakes her head. "I just studied it in school," she said. "He was the real musician." She laughs lightly. "I keep thinking about advice he gave my class. He told us that musicians don't need to see shrinks. The music, he said, is the only therapy you'll ever need. Of course, he never explained how that worked for Cobain, or Janis Joplin."

"Have you thought about seeing a counselor?" I ask.

Olivia kicks at the snow. "No. But I did bring out my old acoustic the other day, started playing a Sister Hazel song. It was one of the only ones I could still play now, with my calluses gone. He taught it to me. I remembered playing it with him and singing the high part." She sniffs and rubs her nose. "I had to

63

stop halfway through. I wanted to break my guitar. I wanted to smash it into a million pieces."

I realize that we've arrived at the garden gate. The sun is completely gone now.

"I'm tired," she finally says. "I think I'd better go."

I walk Olivia to her car. She places her hand on her car door, then turns around and looks me in the eye. "My husband's name was Ralph," she says.

I'm quiet for a moment. "Ralph Bendrix," I say aloud.

"No," she says. "Bendrix is my name."

It's especially quiet at the office the next day. Daryl is early as ever, but completely unreceptive to attempts at conversation. I wonder if he could be this bitter about me turning him down for drinks last night, and I make a mental note to invite him out sometime next week. Submissions come in slowly, and we spend most of the day staring at our computer screens. Around four Daryl announces that he's leaving early.

A few minutes after Daryl leaves I realize he's forgotten to turn off his computer. As I reach around the monitor for the power button, I see a single minimized tab at the bottom of his screen. I bring it up. Daryl is three-fourths of the way through a SelfTerminate.com survey.

Extreme sensitivity to sharp objects, but not opposed to gun use. Mild vertigo at elevations higher than two hundred feet. Has no trouble swallowing pills. Is this the Daryl Kaminski I've worked with every day for the past three years? Is this what he boils down to—a list of fears and phobias and preferences?

I'm at the corner table of the deserted bar drinking whiskey. I hate the taste of whiskey, but its burning in my throat feels right—a punishment for missing what must have been numerous signs. Until tonight I had written off his recent moodiness as a phase, a hermit crab's temporary drawing inward. The phrase "cries for help," a remnant from some pamphlet of the past, is playing a loop in my head.

Daryl sounds confused when I call him to invite him to the bar. "I thought you were going out with that girl again" he says. His tone is not accusing, it's baffled, as though he's forgotten that anyone in the world would want to hang out with him. A possibility occurs to me more frightening than the possibly missed signals: that the cries for help have altogether stopped.

In the years we've been running this site, Daryl and I have never spoken to each other about what our own suicides might entail. The problem is not, obviously, that we lacked the imagination. It occurs to me now that for the past three years, we have been running in place, Wile E. Coyote-style, off the edge of a cliff. To plan for ourselves, even in jest, what we so cavalierly suggested to others, would be tantamount to looking down. Reading over The Survey, as I can now only think of it, I feel as though my legs have stopped pumping, and the whistling I can hear in my ears indicates nothing but the thump at the end of a long, hard fall.

It takes Daryl almost an hour to get to the bar. I watch the clock and stir the ice in my glass until it melts.

"How's it going?" I greet him brightly as he walks through the door.

Daryl just shrugs. "Fine."

Shit. This is going to be harder than I thought.

It's a late realization to have just as Daryl sits down at the bar, but I have never had this talk before. With anyone. I haven't even come close. How the hell does one approach a friend of six years and ask if he's thinking of jumping off a building?

I should have kept those suicide leaflets from high school.

Then of course I think of desperately happy Nora Wilmington passing them out in the junior lounge, and I think of her, eight years later, probably in some one-bedroom just like mine, sending out desperate emails to Mayfield classmates, hoping maybe it will be enough if someone just remembers her.

"Daryl," I say. "I think I'm going to that reunion after all."

Daryl looks perplexed for a moment. "But your girlfriend

broke up with you," he says. "You won't have a date."

"Oh yes I will," I say, making, for the second time this week, a Grand Drunk Gesture. "You're coming with me. You are my date."

He doesn't even think about it. "Absolutely not."

"Hey come on," I say, worried because this is one of the few times in my life I've actually seen Daryl look angry. "It'll be a good time. We'll blow off the jocks and hit on their girlfriends. We'll get roaring drunk and see if Mrs. Curtis is still around. Remember her? She broke her arm." My voice trails off at the end because I can see Daryl gripping his beer bottle, not picking at the label like usual, holding tight to it like he's thinking about hitting me.

When he speaks his breath is level. "I hate getting drunk," he says. "You're the one who likes getting drunk." His voice rises. "High school was one of the worst times of my life. I'm not going back so you can act like an ass and brag about the website."

"I'm not going to brag about the website." I feel small, like I'm the one being dragged back to high school.

"What else do you have to talk about?" This hurts the most and he's not even angry now; he's cold, factual. "It was your brilliant idea. It was the only good idea you ever had, and then you had to drag me into it."

"Daryl," I say, practically pleading, amazed this has gone wrong so quickly. "I just wanted your help. I never meant to drag you into anything."

Daryl takes a gulp of beer, considers it, and takes another. "I never can say no to anything," he says. "Not if I think I'm needed."

"I do need you," I say, but it sounds so weak, a half-assed attempt at amends. He looks at me with disgust, as if to say, "Really?" I want very badly to tell him that I know about The Survey and ask if he's all right. But I've been attacked and my base instincts are up, and this wounded and childish part of my brain wants to go back to denying The Survey, denying Olivia and Ralph and a kid from Michigan who isn't even a teenager yet.

Daryl breaks the silence. "I should go," he says. "I shouldn't have said all that. I'm sorry." He sounds very, very tired, as if he has unloaded himself of a burden that already wore him down too much.

This would be the time to reach out and stop him, to look him in the eye and tell him he is my friend, to say, no matter how cliché and trite it sounds, that people care for him and his life is worth living. Instead, shamed to silence by more guilt, I watch as he gets off his stool and walks away.

One week later, I'm in Olivia Bendrix's driveway, helping pack her car. She's traveling light. The rest of her possessions, as well as her husband's things, are in a storage locker in Gahanna. She's telling me about the contents of the locker when tears well up in her eyes and she looks down her driveway. "I'm thinking about throwing away the key," she says.

"You shouldn't," I tell her.

After we load everything I run to my car and grab Olivia's gift out of the backseat. "Oh God," she says, not bothering to hide her distaste as she pulls the gift-shop coat from the packaging. "What is it?"

I'm grinning. "It's a Blue Jacket. See?" I gesture to the hockey logo on the back. "Something to remember the city by."

"Well," she says, "it's very, um, warm-looking." We make eye contact, and there's embarrassed laughter. The silence that follows seems to signal a shift.

"It's not so bad, is it?" I ask. "Columbus?"

She purses her lips. "I think that Columbus is a very young city." She looks at me, a measured stare. "It has promise, but it doesn't quite know what it wants to be yet." She smiles. "And that's not a bad thing."

I nod, swallowing hard. "Well," I say, wondering at which point we stopped talking about the city at all, "don't forget Columbus entirely."

She places her hand on my right shoulder and gives it a squeeze. "Thank you."

After she gets in the driver's seat and buckles up, I tap on the window. Like an idiot, still trying to stay casual, I ask, "Do you think you'll come back here someday?"

She looks at the jacket on the driver's seat and gives a sad smile.

"Probably not."

That night, around four in the morning, I call Daryl.

"What's going on?" He sounds like his usual mumbling self. I have already steeled my resolve before making this phone call. No matter how asleep he is, I will not apologize and tell him to go back to sleep.

"I want you to come to the office," I say.

"Are you drunk?" he asks, and I wonder, have I done this to him before? For this late-night call, though, I am stone sober, realizing the powerlessness of alcohol in the face of the long-term guilt that lies before me.

"Just come in," I say. "I want to show you a recommendation I wrote up."

I make the drive slowly, even though the lights on High Street all blink yellow and traffic is nonexistent. Some nights at this hour, the street still simmers with vagrants finishing forties and college kids out too late, but tonight I see none of them. The streets are empty and, I cannot help but think, pure.

Daryl, of course, has beaten me. He sits in his chair, bleary-eyed and in pajama pants. For a moment it's like we're back in the dorms, nearing the end of a late-night session of studying and pizza.

"What's this all about?" he asks, more tired than anything.

"The twelve-year-old," I say. "I finished his recommenda-tion." I hand the sheet to Daryl. "Tell me what you think."

Daryl takes the paper and looks at it for a long time. He nods and hands the paper back to me. "I think it's good," he says.

"One of the better ones in recent memory."

He smiles. "I'd say so."

The recommendation, a variant of the one I gave to Olivia right before she pulled out of the driveway, a rough draft of what we would, in a few minutes, send to every user in the site's history, is this:

-Go to high school.

-Go to college (but not U. of M.).

-Live your life.

When we send the last one out to the last user, we terminate SelfTerminate.com.

There is nothing dramatic, really, about the deletion of a website. Daryl types in a few commands on the keyboard, the server makes a restrained rattling noise. The sun, of course, begins to rise as soon as we've finished, and it slowly fills the room with light.

And in a few hours or days, the morbid and macabre citizens of the Internet flip a tab on their browsers and wonder: *What's going on with SelfTerminate.com?* They go back and look a couple times, some of them, but within a week or so the whole enterprise is forgotten, barely a footnote in forgettable Internet history. Those who know the site existed at all shake their heads and wonder: *Did they get in trouble? Did they lose their nerve? Whatever happened to the Suicide Guys?*

Brenda Layman

Brenda Layman is a freelance writer and prolific member of many Central Ohio writers' groups.

Born in Ashland, Kentucky, Brenda has lived most of her life in the Columbus, Ohio area. She is a graduate of The Ohio State University and is currently working on a Master of Communication and Marketing degree at Franklin University.

Brenda and her husband, Mark, have a small internet business called Select Authors which develops and promotes indie authors and provides website design and management services to small businesses.

Although she has published many award-winning articles on topics related to outdoor recreation and wellness, "A Fish Story" is her first foray into published fiction. The story was inspired by her husband's encounter with an eccentric fisherman on the Big Walnut River.

Along with author and life coach Jerry Lopper, Brenda edits an online writers' group, Fiction Writers' Platform. Brenda is also an avid fly angler, a reluctant gym rat, an enthusiastic cook, and a happy bibliophile with full bookshelves who has discovered the infinite storage capacity of e-readers.

Read her blogs at www.select-authors.com.

A FISH STORY
By Brenda Layman

"I've been catching crappies all morning. I ain't never seen 'em like that. They jumped out of the water—ten, twelve feet— and threw the hook. Every time."

The man took a sip of beer. He looked quite ordinary sitting there in his folding canvas chair on the riverbank. The tattoos on his forearms were ordinary tattoos of snakes and initials. A small silver earring sparkled at his right earlobe, and his longish hair stuck out from under a ball cap, tunnel-shaped brim pulled low over his eyes. His clothes were ordinary: jeans and a T-shirt, and flip-flops on his feet. He reclined a little in the chair, right ankle on left knee, and held an unremarkable can of beer in his left hand and a fishing rod in his right.

I had asked him, "Any luck?" the way every fisherman salutes another fisherman on the river.

My first impulse was to assume the man was a raving drunk, but his words lacked the telltale slur of inebriation. Leaping crappies? Was he joking? If so, he had the most deadpan delivery I'd ever heard. I tried to see the expression on his face, but the ball cap hid most of it. I could feel his gaze on me, though, and I replied, "Is that so? Wow, that must have been something."

"Yep. Was."

His line drooped across the slow green water to a red and white bobber. He pulled it up, either to check his bait or to show me how he had hooked those acrobatic crappies. There was no bait. He had rigged a jig and spinning lure about a foot under the bobber, with a lead weight snugged up under the bobber instead of down by the lure. I'd never seen such a strange way of fishing. The man swung the rig back out over the water, and when the bobber was resting on the surface he relaxed into his canvas chair and took another sip of beer.

"Well," I said, "I'm going to go down the river a way and

see if anything is biting."

"I saw an alligator down there a while ago," he replied.

This was the Big Walnut River in Columbus, Ohio, not the Florida Everglades.

"Did you say an alligator? Maybe it was a snapping turtle."

"Nope, it was a 'gator, all right. I got a real good look at the head when it reared up out of the water. Just a little 'un, maybe four or five feet long."

He was crazy, of course, a harmless madman who spent his time drinking beer on the riverbank and fantasizing about wild adventures. I thanked him and walked on down the bank.

Just where the river began a slow turn to the south, I could see a place that looked promising. It took me several minutes to pick my way along among the rocks and mud, careful not to slip and break my expensive fly rod or any part of myself. I was a much more impetuous angler in my youth, scrambling over rocks and crawling through underbrush, but if there's one thing I've learned over the years it's that the fish will either be there or they won't. No amount of hurrying will change that.

A spot of bright red protruded from the vegetation at the river's edge, followed by a splash of yellow, and then a flash of bright blue. Kayaks, a whole flotilla of them, were ready to launch from exactly the place where I planned to wade. I heard the voices of the boaters, heard laughter and chatter and small squeals as they slipped on the muddy bank. One by one they slid their narrow crafts into the water and paddled around, waiting for the entire group to gather before taking off down the river. There were six of them, each a different color—red, yellow, blue, green, orange, and purple, like brightly colored water birds both in hue and volume. It would be a while before the fish, chased into hiding by all the commotion, would venture from their hiding places along the rocky shore.

By the time I reached the bend in the river, the kayakers had moved along until they appeared as a small, rainbow-colored cluster at the furthest point still visible to me down the river. Strangely, they didn't disappear around the next bend, but hovered just at the edge of my vision.

I soon forgot them as I stepped into the river and prepared to cast, balancing my felt-soled boots on the submerged rocks. I tied on a Muddler Minnow, often my first choice of searching pattern, cut the four-pound test line with my knife, then closed the knife and clipped it onto my pocket. I'd see what kind of response I got, and then choose subsequent flies accordingly.

I heard someone calling and looked up the river. The other fisherman was standing up, pointing to the riverbank opposite me, and yelling something I couldn't hear. He put down the beer and the fishing rod and cupped his hands around his mouth to amplify his words.

"That's where I saw the 'gator!"

I waved to let him know I'd heard his warning, if a warning it was meant to be. *Crazy guy*, I thought.

I cast into the slow green water near the bank, and I was immediately rewarded with a pull at the end of my line. It was a small green sunfish, sparkling like a jewel in the late afternoon sun. A satisfied laugh escaped me at the prospect of an afternoon spent pulling sparkling fish out of a green river.

I lost the Muddler on the next cast, snagged in the brush behind me. I opened my fly box and examined the contents: another Muddler, two Woolly Buggers, a marabou streamer, two foam ants, and two deer-hair terrestrials. I selected a foam ant and tied it on, ceremonially twisting the hair-thin line six times before pushing the end through the resulting loop and then back again. I brought the line to my mouth to apply the lick of spit that would lubricate it when I slid the knot into perfect tightness.

A shadow moved across the water, and the roar of a jet crossing overhead reminded me that an airport encroached upon the parkland surrounding the river. The sound subsided, and I was left with the rustle of wind, the cries of birds, and the delicate buzz of black dragonflies that hovered along the water's edge. I confess that I glanced now and then at the opposite bank, scanning it for anything reptilian.

I cast again and caught another of the green sunfish. Each cast produced a fish, and each fish was a little bigger and a little prettier than the last. The tenth fish was the biggest sunfish I had ever seen, bigger than my hand. The fly rod bent and danced as the fish struggled against the line. I decided to try for bigger fish in deeper water, and changed to the marabou streamer.

Wading out a little farther, I noticed that the rocks under my boots were becoming more slippery. I could still see the kayaks in the distance and wondered briefly why they had not continued down the river, but when I cast the marabou streamer into the slow current and began to strip it back, all my attention centered on the end of my line. A fish hit the streamer hard, then powered its way upward to break the surface in a spectacular leap. It was a crappie, silver and black, thrashing in the air as it flung the hook away and dropped back into the water. I looked at the wake spreading in concentric circles where the fish had disappeared. A crappie. A crappie that leaped ten feet out of the water and threw the hook. Anyone could tell you that just doesn't happen.

I cast again. The rocks became slicker and my balance more precarious with every step. Another strike, and another crappie flung itself out of the water and shook itself free. I took another step, this time onto a rock that shifted under my weight. My right boot slid forward and I sought frantically for a solid place to put my left one, nearly going down, but finally righting myself.

Pulling the line up for another cast, I saw a glint of movement at the end and looked closer to see that the marabou streamer was no longer a thing crafted of thread and feathers, but a lively minnow with a streak of red down its side.

As if in a dream, I cast the minnow, once, then again, and felt another strike. This time the fish that burst into view was a brown trout, as long as my arm. It happened slowly, but not in slow motion—rather as if time had become elastic, stretching
74

the moment so that I had time to marvel over the way the gorgeous speckled creature flexed its body, how water sprayed from it in drops that caught the long evening rays of the sun.

The great trout slapped the water and disappeared, and the line went slack. It had to be a dream, I thought, but dreams don't splash and sparkle. Dreams don't sound and smell and feel as real as what I was experiencing.

I stepped back on the shifting, slippery rocks and brought the rod back for another cast, but the line hit something behind me. I turned to see that the sloping, wooded bank was gone. Behind me was a steep wall of rock, layers of ocher and umber stone rising far above my head. A rock wall rose before me on the other side of the river, too. Somehow I had waded into a different place where the river ran through a deep canyon.

I cast again and again, hooking one after another of the fantastic trout. Each one powered itself into the air, shaking the hook from its mouth and falling back into the water with a tremendous splash. The four-pound line should have snapped long ago, but it held, and I knew that it would not, *could* not, break. Dream world or not, I had never fished like that, and I wanted more of it.

Another shadow crested the rock wall and moved over the water. I saw movement reflected on the water's surface and expected to see the stiff outline of a plane from the nearby airport. Instead I saw wings that moved, and a long, cylindrical body. I looked up to see a dragonfly the length of a telephone pole, and I heard the deafening whirr of its wings as it dipped and dove. I ducked away from it, but there were more of them, moving over the water and through the canyon in a swarm. The slimy rocks pitched and moved under my feet, but still I wanted more, and I cast again.

The power of the strike nearly ripped the fly rod from my grasp. I fought to stay upright and cowered under the droning, swooping giants filling the canyon overhead, but I held on to the rod. In the instant before the creature broke the surface, I knew what it was.

The alligator thrust itself out of the shallows, tail thrashing, mouth gaping wide and showing an array of deadly teeth. Its breath stank of the fish and mammals it had devoured, and it roared with rage at the tiny hook set into the flesh at the corner of its jaw. It spun onto its back in the death roll that alligators use to drown their prey, and still the four-pound line did not break.

I dropped the rod and turned to run, but there was nowhere to go. The red rock wall rose behind me. My fingernails bent and broke as I clawed at the vertical surface in desperate, mindless panic. Then I felt the line tighten around my ankle and realized it was tangled around my boot. The alligator jerked its head, and I fell into the mud and felt myself begin to slide over the slimy rocks and into the deeper water.

All around the alligator I had hooked they were gathered, not brightly-hued kayaks, but six multi-colored killers, all waiting for their brother to deliver the feast. Red, blue, yellow, green, orange, and purple; each of them with a huge, open mouth full of yellow teeth and each stinking of death.

My hand groped for my knife, but it was gone. Somehow I had dropped it in the struggle. I seemed locked in time that continued in that stretched-out fashion all around me. The alligators, the water, the rocks, and the line around my ankle that finally pulled me completely under all proceeded as if they had always been in motion. I tried to force myself awake, but knew with horrible certainty it was no dream. Just before my head went under I heard, above the ominous drone of the giant dragonflies, the sound of a man's screams reverberating off the canyon walls.

My eyes were open, and I saw through the muddy water a glint of steel among the green-coated rocks—my knife. Slowly, it seemed, my hand stretched toward it; my fingers grasped it, flipped it open, and my body arced toward my foot, toward the mouth of the creature that was ready to kill me. I sliced the

76

blade through the water and felt it open the flesh of my leg just above my boot top. I sliced again and felt the line go slack. Crawling, kicking, gasping for air, I clawed my way out of the river and onto the bank, expecting with every breath to feel sharp teeth rip into me.

My breathing slowed, and I opened my eyes to blue sky above me. An airplane crossed high above, leaving its white contrail behind. I heard the soft buzz of dragonflies flitting in the weeds near my head. I sat up. The canyon walls were gone. My hand still gripped the knife, and my fly rod lay on the bank, half in the water. I stood and picked it up. The marabou streamer was gone, and the four-pound line with no weight at the end fluttered in the soft breeze. I looked down the river, but the kayaks were gone. Upriver, the fisherman had also disappeared, and it was getting dark.

Blood trickled from a shallow wound on my leg and my hands were scraped and bloody. It was real, as real as anything I've ever experienced. I had the wounds to prove it, but the red canyon walls, the alligators, the giant insects, and the only witness were gone.

I emerged from the wooded margin near the parking lot just as a car carrying the day's last picnickers went by. The woman in the passenger seat glanced at me, her brief smile indicating a flicker of interest in my sodden appearance.

"Did you fall in?" she asked.

"No," I answered.

I wanted to tell her what had happened. I wanted someone to tell me they believed me, to know I wasn't crazy. Then I realized how it would sound, that she would think me insane, or drunk, or both. Better to just walk away. Better to look like just an ordinary fisherman.

David Meeks

David Meeks began reading scary young adult fiction at an early age. By the age of twelve, he moved on to Stephen King. About the same time, the desire to create through the written word had planted itself firmly in his mind.

Now nearly thirty-four, David enjoys reading and writing more than ever, and in a broad variety of genres. When writing he follows one simple rule: if the story is not already completely fantastical or absurd, then keep trying. He is currently working on a novel for young adults that features cats and an incredible journey, as well as a medieval fantasy novel. He hopes that both will find a publisher once they are finished.

David obtained a B.A. in English at The University of Findlay, where he found endless support from his instructors in his creative abilities. There he created a lengthy parody which pulled together a few of Shakespeare's plays and tied them all to an eccentric psychiatrist far in the future. Now completely reworked for this anthology, David hopes you enjoy his absurd glimpse into the future.

He would like to thank everyone in the CCC who helped inspire this more approachable version of Dr. Butte's story, as well as his wife Deborah for her constant support, his parents for giving him fingers to type with, and his friend Sara for bringing this project to his attention.

THE ROOTS OF MADNESS
By David Meeks

The year was 2090. Dr. Bill Butte had been in his office on the 154th floor of the Shaky Spear Home for the Criminally Insane in Columbus, Ohio since six o'clock that morning. Security Officer Clyde Williams had no idea what that man did all day, every day, in his office, but it wasn't Clyde's business to know. His job was to stand guard in the hallway and occasionally break up a fight amongst the patients; that, in addition to sitting in his trusty yellow chair just down the hall from Dr. Butte's office, was all that was required of him.

The doctor's tendency to sequester himself for large portions of the day was a common occurrence, and Clyde thought nothing of this for the first few years of Dr. Butte's employment. But one day about three years ago, Clyde noticed a penny in front of the doctor's door and bent over to pick it up. The penny slid under the doctor's door before he could touch it. It had somehow been *sucked* inside the old man's office, where a loud pop, similar to that of a distant fireworks show, issued from within. Since that day, Clyde had never received a reply after knocking on the doctor's door. But Clyde made a daily habit of setting a penny on the floor just to see it get sucked under. It was the highlight of his day.

Clyde straightened himself as the elderly doctor finally emerged from his office, his clean, white coat in shocking contrast with the dull browns and mustard yellows of the aged décor. Butte's hair was a white, frizzy mess that wrapped around his head, framing a bald scalp riddled with liver spots. The man's most arresting feature—in Clyde's opinion at least— was his eyes. A vision correction surgery gone wrong had left him cross-eyed, with one eye looking slightly up, and the other looking slightly down.

After locking his office door, Dr. Butte shuffled down the dimly lit hallway, with token clipboard tucked under his right arm, and approached his trusty security officer.

"Found that person yet?" asked Dr. Butte as he straightened his tie.

"Oh, the one with the pennies?" said Clyde with as much innocence as he could muster. "No. I…I'm sorry doctor. They must know when my breaks are…" He felt foolish for lying to the old man.

Dr. Butte held up a penny for Clyde to inspect. "Not that I mind someone giving me money," Butte said, "I just want to know who makes a ritual out of…well, this." He held the penny closer to Clyde's face.

"Seems pretty silly to me, sir," Clyde said, at a loss for much else to say. The doctor checked his clipboard, nodded to Clyde, and continued down the corridor one penny richer.

Clyde stared after the man for a moment, regretting his own petty lies. After all, the doctor was always courteous to him, and even conversed with him daily, if in a distracted sort of way. It was nice to have some company on the job, especially since the two of them (aside from the weekly cleaning lady), were the only staff members on this floor. One day Clyde would 'fess up to his penny-watching antics, but for now he smiled and followed the doctor.

The Heavy Security Wing sat beyond a handful of rooms and locked metal doors. The doctor spent most of his time with these more "extreme cases," as he called them. Clyde supposed he understood why—the more "extreme" the case was, the more time it would take to help that patient. Something about the doctor's reactions to these cases, though, seemed strange to Clyde. Dr. Butte would invariably exit the patient's cell in remarkably good humor, and would rave about the patients' stories and how much he enjoyed them, all the while scribbling frantically on his clipboard as if he were afraid of forgetting something. Never once did Clyde hear Dr. Butte speak of curing the patients; it was always "story" this and "fascinating" that. Such things were beyond Clyde's comprehension, however, and he merely assumed the old doctor was doing the best he could. If something seemed slightly *off* to Clyde, he merely shrugged and went about his day. He shrugged often.

Clyde and the doctor stepped inside the foyer of the Heavy Security Wing, and the rusty, metal door groaned shut behind them. Six doors lay in wait ahead of them—the first four occupied with a fresh set of patients, the other two to be occupied by the end of the day.

"Soooo…," the doctor began, holding his clipboard just a few inches from his gaunt face, "starting from the left we have a Mr. Fred Lear." The doctor gasped suddenly. "Ah, yes! Fred Lear! 'King of the Artificial Community,' is what I believe he called himself." He leaned ever so slightly toward Clyde and continued his exposition in a whisper. "This man was wealthy beyond anything we could imagine, Clyde. Any of those robotic people you see around the city, whose job it is to clean for people, babysit, walk the family dog, all of those were created by the man behind that door."

"Mmmm." Clyde gave his best falsetto to show he understood the importance of this patient.

"Mmmm, indeed," said the doctor, no longer whispering. "I believe we have two new charges coming today as well, Clyde. A young man and young woman, are they?"

Clyde nodded and said, "Yes, Dr. Butte. The first one should be here by now so I'll go fetch him while you're in with Mr. Lear. You don't think he's dangerous, do you?"

"Mr. Lear?" the doctor guffawed. "He's even older than I am. In fact the only reason I wanted him in this wing was for convenience—can't spend all day walking back and forth, you know."

"Okay, Doctor." Clyde was not fond of leaving the doctor alone with the patients, for safety's sake, but he sounded confident about Mr. Lear. "I'll be back within the next hour. Good luck in there." Dr. Butte muttered what sounded like "indeed" as Clyde handed him the keys to Lear's cell and then made his way to the elevator.

Dr. Butte spent nearly an hour with Mr. Lear—an hour well spent, Clyde guessed, as he emerged looking as giddy as a child with a new toy.

"Clyde!" the doctor exclaimed, gripping his clipboard with both hands. "Mr. Fred Lear bestowed his wealth among his daughters, and then was betrayed by them! He went absolutely mad when they threw him out of their homes, leaving him with nothing but the rags on his back. Isn't that..."

His sentence ended in a weak croak as he looked up to see Clyde gripping a forlorn young man by the arms.

"Doctor," Clyde said in a nearly breathless whisper, his large nose wrinkled and eyes welling with tears. "You want this guy in cell five?"

Dr. Butte nodded a "yes" to Clyde's question and then it hit him—the young man smelled as if he had tripped into a vat of cheap men's cologne. The doctor took one hand off his clipboard and buried his nose in the sleeve of his coat.

"Good Jesus, Clyde, and in a hurry!" he exclaimed.

The young man did not put up a fight, and tumbled to the floor of his padded cell. Clyde slammed the door behind him.

"And who is that, then?" asked the doctor.

"Um," Clyde stammered as he looked at the patient's file. "Rah-mee...Rah-moo...I've never seen a name like it, Doctor. How would you say that?"

Dr. Butte took the file for inspection. "Romeo Montague." He smiled thoughtfully. "Quite a name if I do say so myself. Have you any idea why he smells like the floor of a perfume shop?"

Clyde shrugged. "I heard he has a lady friend, who happens to be coming in later today. Could be he was trying to impress her."

"Hmm, very astute of you, Clyde," the doctor said. "I'm anxious to meet them both. Now, however, we must press on. The time, Clyde?"

"One-thirty, Doctor."

"Very well," said Butte as he turned to face cell number two. He repositioned the papers on his clipboard. "Here we have a man named Ham, short for Hamlet. No last name is given, but it does state he is from Denmark, South Carolina. Apparently Ham claims that his uncle murdered his father over some sort of land dispute, and Ham nearly killed his uncle, seeking revenge, multiple times." Butte read a bit more to himself, his thin lips quivering with excitement, then concluded, "And he says he knows his uncle is guilty because his father's ghost told him so!"

"Wow, he sounds cra—"

Clyde paused as the doctor's eyes shot up at him—or rather, above and below him. "I mean, I hope you can help him, Doctor."

"Help? Ah, oh yes!" Dr. Butte laughed. Clyde shrugged and the doctor continued, "I can't help him standing here, though. Can you get the door, Clyde?"

Clyde unlocked the door, which groaned on its rusty hinges like every other door in the facility. The doctor stepped into the cell. "Welcome to Columbus, Ham! Seems things didn't quite work out for you in South Carolina."

Clyde shut the door as the doctor spoke, ready to intervene if the patient became uncooperative. A couple of times, he checked in after hearing the patient raise his voice, but the doctor claimed he was just fine, and emerged unscathed nearly forty-five minutes later. It was no surprise to Clyde when he saw the doctor ecstatic with the results from this patient.

He was prepared to listen to the doctor's usual brief analysis when an announcement came squawking from the outside hallway: "Clyde Williams, please report to patient pick-up immediately." The call repeated another three times before another voice erupted from Romeo's room.

Clyde hurried over to cell number five and unlocked the tiny latch on a small swinging door set at eye level. A set

83

of somber eyes met the security officer's. "They're bringin' my Juliet up here, ain't they?" The young man wailed like a bereaved mother into the other side of the door, tears welling in his eyes. His voice became a hoarse scream.

"I've gone and taken that poison 'cause I thought she was dead, and she's still alive, isn't she?"

"Did he say poison?" Dr. Butte asked. "Clyde, open this door immediately! We must administer..."

Clyde began to reach for his keys, but Romeo's eyes were already sinking out of sight. The two of them could hear the man's body drop to the padded floor below. Clyde opened the door and the doctor confirmed his suspicion.

"Oh, Doc..."

Dr. Butte hung his head as he knelt next to the body. "Quite a shame, Clyde. When you go retrieve who I can only assume is this man's Juliet, could you alert the morgue we'll need him picked up?"

"Certainly, Doctor." Clyde felt a lump rise in his throat, and coughed, quiet as he could, until it passed. "I'll be right back."

Clyde walked briskly, reminding himself that things like this were bound to happen in his line of work. Thankfully, deaths were few and far between on the 154th floor of the Shaky Spear, and he was always able to remain calm and detached. Now, however, Clyde would be forced to escort the dead man's girlfriend upstairs and place her in the cell adjacent to where her Romeo had just died. He visited the morgue to inform them of the death upstairs, collected the young Juliet, and steeled himself for the trouble ahead.

Romeo may have smelled bad, and his clothes were torn in a few places for reasons unknown, but Juliet was an absolute mess. She wore a pink dress stained with what Clyde hoped was only dirt. Her hair was disheveled to the point that Clyde would have laughed if the situation weren't so grim. And her red lipstick had been smeared across the left side of her face.

84

The young lady was cooperative for the entire walk to her cell, and even said a polite "Hello" to Dr. Butte when they arrived, however, Romeo's cologne still hung in the warm, stale air of the Heavy Security Wing, and Juliet became all questions and tears when she caught a whiff of it.

After roughly five minutes, Clyde calmed her down enough that she agreed to enter her room and get some rest before seeing her Romeo, whom she still believed to be alive. He hated himself for lying to her in such a way, but the more control he and the doctor had over the situation the better.

"Dean from the morgue should be up to get you-know-who real soon, Doctor." Clyde whispered this, still just outside Juliet's door.

"Thank you, Clyde, though I'm sure it will be longer than 'real soon.' Dean is not known for being punctual, or anything else for that matter." Dr. Butte turned to face cells number three and four, and sighed into his clipboard. "Looks as though we have two patients left, Clyde. Not counting our teary-eyed young lady, that is."

He tapped his pen on the back of the clipboard, and spoke slowly. "We have a Tim Bevins, who was brought here last night after setting fire to The Athenian—a very upscale apartment complex; and then we have a Mrs. MacBeth, who apparently convinced her husband to commit murder and is now suffering from feelings of immense guilt and is a danger to herself and others. Very intriguing."

Clyde was about to crack a joke about flipping a coin to decide who the doctor should see next, when a great wail issued from cell number six—Juliet's room. She yelled something unintelligible until she ran out of breath. Once Clyde was certain she had finished, he opened the miniature door to peek inside. Just as he leaned forward, an arm thrust through the door and a finger nearly poked through his left eye socket. Clyde grasped the girl's wrist to subdue her arm, and found her to be surprisingly strong as she jerked to the left and right.

COLUMBUS CREATIVE COOPERATIVE

"Calm down!" He yelled over and over until she withdrew her arm.

"Please, let me see him." She whimpered from somewhere off to the side. "It's been so long." They could barely hear her voice, and Clyde caught himself as he began to lean toward the door again—he settled for an arm's length away.

"Doctor, what should we do?" he whispered as Dr. Butte joined him.

"Perhaps we should tell her the truth?" the doctor mused, tapping his pencil lightly on his clipboard.

Clyde, horrified at first, recomposed himself and nodded in agreement. "It does seem like the right thing to do, I suppose. They're still people, even though they have these...problems."

"It's the human condition at work before our very eyes, Clyde."

"I suppose so, doctor," he replied, only partially understanding. "Should we open the cell?"

Dr. Butte nodded, and Clyde opened the door, which groaned in unison with the young woman sitting cross-legged on the floor. She looked up at the unlikely duo, the front of her dress dark with moisture. "Young lady," began the doctor as he knelt just outside her doorway, "Mr. Montague...Romeo, that is, seems to have ingested some poison before his arrival here and is now..."

He did not need to finish his sentence. The young woman cried silently for a moment, her face buried in her hands, and the doctor and Clyde let her mourn, watching for any sudden, violent movements. None came, and she finally asked the inevitable question: "Can I see him, please?"

They both knew it was certainly far from protocol, but they couldn't deny her at a time like this. Clyde unlocked Romeo's cell door and Juliet lunged at her boyfriend, hugging his body as the man's cologne attacked the air in force once again.

In an unexpected turn, the girl looked up at Clyde and the doctor and said, "We was in love, but our families didn't want us together. I heard someone told my Romeo that I died inna accident, an' I wanted to get to him, to tell him I was okay, but my family had me brought here before I could." She laughed dryly and said, "Kinda funny that his family committed him at the same time, huh? Kinda like it was meant to be," she sucked in her bottom lip. "Only he's dead now, an' I got no one except you two." She shook her head violently. "Well I don't *want* you two!" Then, quicker than a penny being sucked under a door, Juliet hiked up her dress and pulled what might have been a letter opener from the top of her right stocking.

Clyde was a big man, and certainly strong, but he was unfortunately as slow as his wits. One moment, the girl in the pink dress was hugging her beloved Romeo, the next second she had one arm around Dr. Butte, while the other hand plunged the sharpened piece of metal into the doctor's stomach.

"Doctor!" Clyde yelled, as he pried the girl off the old man and sent her reeling back into Romeo's cell. As she flew back, the blade remained in her grasp and drops of blood spurted from the doctor's stomach. Dr. Butte gasped quietly and fell to his knees, one hand over his wound, while Juliet, without hesitation, turned the blade on herself, piercing her own heart as she gazed down at her boyfriend. She breathed heavily for a moment, mouthing incoherent laments, and finally went limp as her last breath escaped into the foul, cologne-drenched air.

"Clyde," said the doctor with surprising firmness, "take me back to my office, would you?"

Clyde protested. The old man surely needed medical assistance.

"No, Clyde, it's too late. I can feel that it's too late. Now I need you to do something very important for me, and in a hurry, but we *must* return to my office first."

Clyde didn't hesitate. First, he retrieved a towel from a supply closet and tied it firmly around the old man's middle in order to slow the bleeding. Then, he scooped him up, kicked shut the door to cell number five, and walked back to the office he had so longed to see for himself.

Once they arrived at that mysterious, money-eating door, Clyde thought instinctively that he should reach for a penny to set down, and realized with a sinking feeling that those days were now over. What was to occur behind this door would be a final act for the doctor. An *off* sort of feeling struck Clyde then as events began falling into place for him: the doctor's obsession with his patients' stories, the penny and loud popping noise from behind the office door, the doctor's routine of hiding in his office for six hours each day, every day. But still, Clyde did not understand how all these things were connected. He knew, though, that the doctor had been doing something out of the ordinary for the entirety of his employment at the Shaky Spear, and he knew that he was about to find out what.

Despite Clyde's hopes that the doctor's office contained marvels beyond imagining, he found everything to be quite normal. The walls were the same drab yellow that adorned the hallways, the carpeting was dirty brown, and it contained nothing but a small, wooden desk and two metal chairs, as well as a few framed certificates that hung behind the doctor's chair.

Clyde led Dr. Butte to his desk and lowered him gently.

"Have a seat, my friend," offered the doctor, still with a firm voice.

Clyde sat down reluctantly, still concerned for the doctor's condition. Once seated, he was able to get a closer view of the doctor's desk, and a drawing of a young man underneath the glass desktop. "Who's that little guy?" Clyde asked.

Dr. Butte pointed feebly to the picture. "His name is William. I suppose you could say he's my protégé." Clyde raised an eyebrow, and the doctor tried to clarify. "Sort of a student. Well, no, that's not exactly right. I'm doing most of it for him."

The doctor was in obvious pain, but Clyde could see that this was important to the old man, so he humored him.

"Doing what for him, sir?"

"I am helping him become something."

"I see," lied the security officer. "Well, he's a handsome kid. His clothes are kind of strange, though."

"They're sixteenth century. And, yes, he is handsome, but he's a bit older now. Grown into a fine young man, he has." The doctor then opened a drawer, wincing at the motion, and produced a small, metal disc four inches in diameter and one inch thick which he set on the desk in front of him. It was shiny like chrome and had two wires protruding from opposite ends of its circumference, and set into one side was a display with red numbers and six black buttons lined up beside it. Clyde looked at it for a few moments, but couldn't quite see what the purpose of it was. He looked back up and noticed the doctor had grown paler.

"Clyde." The doctor broke the silence. "I am a psychiatrist, but I've had an ulterior motive for working here. I'm interested in helping these people, but I'm even more interested in their stories. You don't read much, do you?"

"No, not really, Doc. Just *The Dispatch*. Well, just the sports section, really."

The old man's brows perked up. "Ah, yes. Go Bucks!" Clyde appreciated the doctor's feeble attempt, but he could see it was forced. The doctor grew even paler in the dim light. "Well, it's okay if you're not much of a reader. I can see that you're a good man, though. And I have appreciated working with you over the years, but it seems my days must end with this. I have one final favor to ask of you before I go. And you must promise to keep this a complete secret. No matter how amazing it may seem, you mustn't tell a soul what I am about to share with you.

"Now listen closely, and I hope you understand, or at least appreciate, my problem. I have been taking our patients' stories and turning them into plays. But not just plays—*sixteenth century* plays! I have fallen in love with this time period over the years, and..."

Clyde watched the doctor trace the edges of the metal disc,

and then remembered where he had seen something like this before. "That's a time machine!" The words burst from his lips before he could control himself, and the doctor shushed him.

"Please don't tell anyone. Jail is the least of my worries right now, but these are still illegal."

"How'd you get that?" Clyde was beside himself.

"I really can't tell you that. I'm sorry. Please let me finish explaining myself." Clyde apologized, and the doctor continued. "That noise you hear from my office each day is this device." He pointed to the disc. "More accurately, it is the matter in the room filling in the space where my body used to be. This is why I don't have a lot of loose knick-knacks in here, because every time I went back in time everything would fly from my shelves." The doctor paused. "I know that you've been responsible for the pennies sliding under my door."

Clyde shifted uncomfortably in his chair.

"It's okay, Clyde. I would have done the same thing. Now, as I said, I have been going back in time, and as you have probably figured out by now, I have been doing this during my office hours.

"I used this time to explore a little place in England, a place called Stratford-on-Avon, and met the most remarkable little boy. Of course, I had to find some clothing before I presented myself to anyone, but that's far from my point. I had become familiar with many of the locals, passing myself off as a somewhat wealthy traveler who passed through that area regularly. Little do they know that I live far in the future, and only visit that one little place." He attempted to laugh at his scheme, but the movement proved too painful, and he continued.

"So I befriended various people, and eventually met this young man named William, whose picture you see on this desk. I took it in secret," he whispered. "He had a love for writing and acting, which I have always loved myself. For years, I've taken bits of patients' stories and given them to him. You can imagine how hard it was relating these stories—these futuristic
90

stories—to this young man from the past. It was exhausting, but well worth it.

"Once I worked these modern stories into the young man's time period, so that he would not think me crazy for talking about robots and such, we both transformed them into plays. It has been the most exhilarating time of my life writing with that young man, but I can no longer go there for...obvious reasons."

Dr. Butte pointed to a cloth sack next to the desk. "And now we come to my favor. In there are exactly one hundred and fifty-four sonnets, of my own creation, as well as basic outlines of many of my patients' cases, that I would like to be delivered to the young William so that he may read them and use them for himself. I need you to deliver these for me tonight."

"You want me to go back in time?" Clyde was beside himself, and a little frightened. He scrambled for something to say as the doctor stared at him. "Does it hurt?"

The doctor chuckled involuntarily and cringed at the pain it caused. He drew a deep breath and said, "Clyde, you really are a character. No, time travel does not hurt."

"Where do I go when I get there? And what about my clothes?"

"I'll explain your first question in just a moment. And as for your clothing, you will be in the Forest of Arden, at night, and only for roughly ten minutes. I've specified a time and place for the young William to pick up my gift—we have a tight schedule worked out—and he will be arriving a few hours after you drop it off. You don't have to worry about running into him."

The doctor asked Clyde to allow him time for some last minute notes and a final goodbye letter to his young friend.

"I can still call for help, Doctor," Clyde said, persisting.

"No, friend, I've done nearly all I wanted to do here. If I live I'll just be put in a home and no better off than Mr. Lear down the hall." The doctor's voice grew weaker. "Half an hour, Clyde, and I will send you off."

The doctor wrote, slowly but with deliberation. Clyde paced the room, occasionally stopping to peer out the window into the hazy air of Columbus. The sun drifted behind the myriad of tall buildings.

Soon, the doctor was finished, and handed Clyde his final notes to be added to the contents of the sack. "I know this is all probably very confusing to you, Clyde, but I appreciate you helping me with this, for this final act validates my entire existence."

"I don't mind at all, Dr. Butte, but, there is one thing. When I get back, you won't be... *here* anymore, will you?"

The doctor sank further into his chair. "Clyde, I will set the machine to bring you back to your own home. And once you leave I will call the head of security here and tell them I sent you home early, and that I foolishly opened Miss Juliet's door on my own. You will be cleared from any wrongdoing." The doctor smiled weakly, and Clyde nodded his understanding. "Now, Clyde, here is what you need to do."

After a few minutes of preparation, Clyde activated the apparatus. The experience wasn't painful—it tingled instead, a sensation which he decided he quite enjoyed. It was strange that he had been standing in an office one minute, and now he was surrounded by trees. The air smelled clean, too—no car fumes in *this* place.

Dr. Butte had given him a flashlight fixed with a blue lens so people would be less likely to spot him in the dark. Clyde followed the pennies wedged into trees until the fifteenth one, which he found easily. The tree had a wide hole in which to fit the bag of sonnets. Clyde couldn't help taking one peek at the inside of the bag before getting rid of it, though. The things the doctor had written looked a little strange, with the "U's" looking more like "V's," and Clyde knew that some things were beyond his understanding.

There was also a letter to the young man, which Clyde read:

William,

Please accept these sonnets as a token of my love and appreciation. Make of their subject what you will.

You will also find the subjects for my final plays which you may rework with your exceptional talents.

I beg of you to make our combined efforts into more than stacks of papyrus. They are better than you may realize.

Yours Eternally,
WFB

Todd Metcalf

Born and raised in Columbus, Ohio, Todd Metcalf attended New Albany High School and The Ohio State University. After graduation, he worked in various technology and executive management positions with some of Columbus's top companies. He currently runs a business consulting company serving the vibrant community in Central Ohio. He is happily married with two wonderful daughters.

With roots firmly planted in the city, it was only logical for Todd to write a story set in Columbus. As one who favors the uncommon path, his take on the anthology's theme is far from traditional.

"Kweezi and Leek Go Shopping" is a near future, dystopian tale of two pre-adolescents who go shopping for a most unique item, not traditionally sold in the local department store. It is a disturbing vision of the future that explores both conservative and liberal biases.

"Kweezi and Leek" is a political satire that Todd is confident you will appreciate.

KWEEZI AND LEEK GO SHOPPING
By Todd Metcalf

There was nothing to do in Columbus.

Despite booming to one of the largest U.S. cities since the Great Expansion, the Ohio city lacked exciting activities. But today was different. Leek was with his best friend, Kweezi, and they weren't interested in entertainment; they were determined to transform their future.

Leek's pale complexion and blond, curly hair were in direct contrast to Kweezi's dark skin and short, cropped hair. Leek's rounded face made him seem younger than his eleven years while Kweezi's rounded nose and sleek face complemented her lean, twelve-year-old body.

"Nice day, isn't it?" a raspy voice asked.

They froze. The unexpected sound was like glass shattering against the empty street. Their heads turned toward the voice. A straggly man, with hair clumped in greasy ropes, greeted them with a full set of pearly whites.

He must have had some money once to get teeth that bright, Leek thought.

The man's flannel shirt and grungy black jeans reeked of putrid refuse; the stench effortlessly traversed the generous buffer zone between them. The man leaned against the old, soot-stained Rhodes Tower, gnawing on a toothpick. The wrinkles in his face deepened as Leek studied him.

"What did you say?" Kweezi inquired, eyeing the man's dubious sense of fashion.

"I don't see many people on the sidewalks these days. I suspect you came out to enjoy this particularly nice day. Columbus is typically overcast."

His saggy eyes revealed the submission they saw in most adults. The strict laws against harming children had their intended effect of keeping them safe. It would be less severe to murder a busload of adults than to lay a violent hand on a child.

Kweezi gathered her composure. "What are you doing out here?"

"I'm just passing the time," he responded, looking amused. *I bet we're the first people you've seen all day,* Leek thought. He didn't want to chat, even though it was a rare opportunity to speak with an adult in person. Their appointment was not for another hour, but he didn't want to cut it close and risk missing their meeting.

"You down on your luck?" Kweezi asked, twisting from Leek's insistent grasp.

The man shrugged with no indication of annoyance.

"Why are you out here?" she demanded.

"I might ask you the same," the old man shot back.

"Are you saying we have no *right* to be out here?" Kweezi said, her hands resting on her hips.

Leek could almost read her thought. *What right do you have to tell us what we can and can't do?*

"No, no, nothing of the sort." The man raised his arms in the air. "Did you consider that I may be as curious to see you out here as you are to see me?"

Leek studied the man's serene face. *He doesn't need to know our business.*

"How about I tell you why I'm here, and you can tell me why you are." He flashed another smile, although not as earnest as before.

Leek knew Kweezi would want to listen, and, being just as inquisitive, he nodded approval against his better judgment.

The man smiled. "I used to be a fraud examiner for the Monetary Clearinghouse. I was good at it, too. I could get around the system like nobody's business. It was something to behold." He pursed his lips, releasing a soft whistle, then modesty regained its tenuous hold over him, "But that was a long time ago."

He looked through Kweezi as though he had found a better place in the distance. "It was in the early days of the Internet, you know," he said, coming back. "Regulators approved Internet commerce via the Clearinghouse once there were enough defenses to ensure ninety-nine point nine percent transaction security. It was the point one percent you had to watch out for, though. Why, if even a tenth of a percent of the total transactions had been fraudulent, it might be a different world today. There'd essentially be no electronic commerce as we know it." He stifled a laugh, aware that he was the only one enjoying the joke. "You might actually *have* to go to a store now and then."

The man's probing eyes seemed to be searching for an expression—any expression—from the two young passersby. Receiving none, he continued, "As you know, once the bots were perfected, they made great fraud examiners, among many other tasks. They single-handedly changed the landscape of the Internet. Overnight, my extensive knowledge became obsolete, and I was out of a livelihood, along with millions of others. The ranks of the unemployed swelled to fantastic proportions within months. That was in 2053, and it led to the greatest depression in the history of the world. Look through your history texts if you think I'm exaggerating. It was the most devastating experience I could imagine."

Leek had learned that the Depression of '53 had devastated the lives of nearly every American. Shortly thereafter, the children's rights laws were passed, which kick-started the Enlightenment period—a rebirth of the modern era. It eventually led to the Great Expansion, arguably the world's most profitable and rewarding age.

"Of course," the man continued. "I looked for other ways to use my skills, but they were no longer portable. I took courses, but the old paradigm was too difficult to break. The artificial intelligence employed by the bots had altered traditional approaches. Most adults were unable to make the intellectual transition." As an afterthought, he added, "It was too much."

Leek stared at him, unable to grasp the intensity of his despair. He glanced at Kweezi, unsure of what to say.

After several moments, the man asked, "What about yourselves?"

Leek responded because long silences made him uncomfortable. He was more trusting of strangers than Kweezi

97

and opened up more easily. "We're going shopping."

"Boy," the older man responded in an admonishing tone, "no one goes *out* shopping—except for one thing." His eyes grew large as he realized their intent.

"That's where we're going," Leek said adamantly. He could see Kweezi getting a little uncomfortable discussing their personal matters.

Apparently understanding their concern, the man turned the discussion back to something more comfortable—himself. "I had a child and a wife once. It was back in the early part of the century, before your time. It was exciting. I had a young wife, a boy who looked up to me..." His grin faded and his eyes momentarily flinched, "But things changed..."

"What did you *do* to them?" Leek asked.

"Oh," the man said as he waived his hand casually, "at the time, I didn't think I did anything. It's only been recently this old mind," he thrust a finger at his forehead, "has understood. As the times changed, I failed to keep up. I came from the old school, so when my wife became interested in a coworker, I didn't like it, not one bit. She was my wife, and I should have..." He became noticeably uncomfortable. "Well, I wouldn't allow her to see him anymore." He scanned the ground for the right words. "I forbid it, actually. She was my *wife!*" He stressed "wife" as though that justified his actions.

"So, she left me. I took her to court because I just couldn't understand how I could be held responsible for not sanctioning her affair. By then, the courts had many cases as precedent against me. The judge automatically gave her custody of my son since I was at fault. Just like that, my family was gone. Then the bots stole my career."

"You gave up," Kweezi accused. "And now you're outside instead of being a productive member of society."

Leek cringed. Kweezi could be ruthless at times.

"No, not just like that," he answered, not defensively, but casually, as though naming off the ingredients of his favorite recipe. "I tried everything until I lost all that I owned. I finally put my life back together once I found the charity down the

98

street."

He pointed to a wreck of a building. Years of neglect and abuse by the elements sanded and pitted the red brick epidermis. The windowpanes that weren't boarded up showed their deep cracks.

"It's a place to sleep. I still don't understand the Internet much, but I've learned enough to get by. I do the jobs young people don't want. I only come out here to get away and think." He swallowed hard and then shook his head quickly as though throwing off the bad memories. "But that's enough about me. What about you? What did your parents do to *you*?" His question seemed sincere.

"They forbid me to go to a concert with my friends," Leek stated.

The man eagerly waited for more but seemed afraid to ask.

Leek obliged. "They tried to make excuses like 'you can't trust people you meet on the Internet' and 'raves cause bad behavior.' Can you believe that? I'm not stupid. I took the necessary precautions by downloading their identification video and matching their voice prints with the government's Identity Base. You can't be more secure than that. Then they tried to say it was too late or I'd miss too much school. Come on, I understand the consequences of my actions and am perfectly willing to accept them. It was just one straw too many. I didn't need parents who constantly infringed upon my rights." A sharp nod added emphasis.

"So you divorced them," the older man said matter-of-factly.

"Straight up."

"Where are they now?" the man asked cautiously.

"They're in jail where they deserve to be." Kweezi sent a laser-edged glare back at him.

The man flinched slightly. "What about your parents?"

"They were violent."

"No adult should hurt a child," the man agreed.

"That's right. They *grabbed* my arm and walked me to my room. It left a red mark for hours."

99

The man clenched his jaw. "I'm sure they deserved whatever they got."

"Looking back, I should have been sent to my room, but brutality can't be tolerated." Fire blazed from Kweezi's eyes.

The man abruptly changed the subject. "So how did you two get together?"

"We met on a social net devoted to helping abused children because our originals punished us unmercifully."

She challenged him with her eyes, but he smiled understandingly.

"You know," she continued, "if a parent stoops to violence, there's no telling what else she may do. While my ex-parents sat in the can to think about what they did, Leek and I became legal siblings. It's been a couple of years now."

"So it's taken you this long to find another set?" inquired the old man, who seemed to be growing sympathetic to their plight.

"We picked another up through the Internet. It was the traditional two-parent configuration. They were great for the first year, really granted us freedom, allowed us to be kids." Kweezi shrugged her shoulders. "Gradually, they changed. They instituted rule after rule until we were bogged down in familial bureaucracy. We were forced to study our school lessons at least an hour a day even though we'd already been connected for an hour of class instruction! They were unreal."

The old man nodded, but Leek could tell he didn't truly agree. The man was just too smart to admit it. *Society will be a whole lot better once everyone realizes that coercion doesn't yield freedom,* Leek thought. But the man admitted he couldn't change, that he was a creature of habit. That's why he was out here, like the other nonconformists.

"We need to go, Kweezi," Leek said, studying his armpad.

Neither of them wanted to miss their appointment with P.S. Parents. They'd scheduled interviews with Kweezi and Leek's three finalists. It was a nearly impossible proposition since parents were becoming scarce, and the choices grew less appealing each year. Fewer adults volunteered despite the generous government subsidies. It was a decidedly difficult issue for the country, with some hoping that the next generation would love children and have the verisimilitude to succeed.

"I wish you luck with your shopping. By the way, do you have any credits you could spare?" the man prodded.

"You know the government won't turn anyone away," Leek said, surmising that the old man had missed the last few Helping HandUps. He had no right to ask a fellow Ohioan for money, especially ones who paid taxes at the sixty-three percent burden on all income and subsidies.

Kweezi and Leek turned and walked away, leaving the man to his thoughts.

They strolled in silence for several blocks, admiring the buildings before them. It was eerie, flitting through a city no longer used as it was designed. They wanted an adventure and eschewed the typical transit system located above the city. Surface transport was no longer efficient; there were too many buildings and not enough land to support adequate transportation, especially since Columbus had become one of the densest cities in the U.S. Most of its structures were built during the Great Expansion in the middle of the century. The surface was the only place to put new buildings, and buildings flourished everywhere physical space was present. Soon, buildings replaced streets and sidewalks. Unfortunately, with the population in alarming decline, many of the buildings were now vacant.

The space between the buildings presented an interesting maze for the occasional pedestrian. The wind whistled and howled eerily through the structural labyrinth. The pad on Leek's arm verified they were slowly closing in on their destination, minutes ahead of schedule.

"I sure don't want a set similar to the old man we just met," Leek offered, to break the silence. "He was too authoritarian for me."

"P.S. wouldn't let someone like him get through anyway. They have one of the best screening procedures of any parental agency," Kweezi assured.

"You're right. I just don't want to get stuck with a bad set for another three years."

Each realized this would not be their last set, regardless of how well they chose. Most children had at least two to three sets before they became teenagers, and in the five teenage years until legal adulthood (and absolute freedom), they would churn at least as many. Each sibling group attempted to beat the odds, but society changed so quickly that adults had difficulty keeping pace. Parents tended to revert to their traditional, dictatorial ways instead of treating children in a civilized manner.

Some teens like Josine and Marty still lived with their birth parents. It never failed to amaze everyone who heard the story. Fourteen and thirteen years old, respectively, they continue habitating with the same parents who brought them into this world, despite the fact that they impose harsh, absurd rules and demand unreasonable conduct, like insisting that they continually be updated of their children's whereabouts. Josine said it wasn't bad since their parents rarely forbid them to go anywhere.

Rarely. Leek and Kweezi thought that was a laugh. Parents who couldn't trust their children put the entire children's rights movement back decades. Despite the harsh discipline, Marty claimed their parents loved them, and they refused to divorce their parents. It wasn't a good tradeoff, in Kweezi's opinion. Teachers routinely counseled Josine and Marty, instructed them of their rights as children and human beings, and explained the simple procedure required to divorce their brutal parents.

Josine and Marty remained unconvinced. Before the current conservative Congress took over, the teachers had the authority to take abused children into custody and file for divorce on their behalf. The discriminatory parents' rights groups forced Congress to pass the law requiring children to file personally. If Kweezi had her way, she would vote the ultra conservatives out and move Congress back to the center. It was important to help children like Josine and Marty who were too brainwashed to help themselves.

102

"Promise me, Leek, that our next parents aren't extreme radicals."

"What do you mean?"

"The teenage years will be the most important years of our lives. It's when we find out who we are."

Leek nodded.

"Our next parents need to allow us to make our own mistakes. Poor choices should be our own responsibility. We have to experience the consequences ourselves because it's the only way to learn in this difficult world."

"Right," Leek said. "It's imperative that they not dictate crucial activities like who we date or what party we go to."

"Exactly. If we bring home a sexual partner or one of the new O.T.C. hallucinogens, there should be no questions, no judgments, no recriminations."

"Did I tell you that Barley pinged me the other day?"

Kweezi shook her head.

"His parents were in his face about his drug use."

"Don't they know that the latest research has proven the drugs don't cause permanent damage?" Kweezi asked

"I know, right? His parents claimed the pharmaceutical companies spent billions for the positive test results."

"Whatever." Kweezi flicked her hand. "It wouldn't matter anyway. A child's body is her own, and the government shouldn't control what she does. Mistakes are part of growing up."

"Totally."

"That's why we make such good sibs, Leek."

Leek punched Kweezi on the arm. No one could ask for a better sib than Kweezi.

They walked until Leek's armband signaled they had arrived.

P.S. Parents occupied the ground floor of an ordinary granite and glass building. If it hadn't been for his pad beeping like a Geiger counter, Leek might have walked right by it without noticing the small 'P.S. PARENTS' sign. A large window underneath vaguely resembled a door. 'PULL' was pasted in even smaller type. Kweezi complied with the instruction and entered without hesitation. Leek preferred to build suspense and double-checked his pad for verification. He reluctantly followed.

Inside, a large chandelier presided over the expansive ceiling in the lobby. A woman, seated behind the reception desk, maniacally pressed buttons on the screens that filled her console. The reception area faced the underground entrance. The receptionist swung her chair around, startled that customers would enter from the street.

"I'm Kweezi, and this is Leek," Kweezi said, pointing to her brother. "We're here to interview our three sets."

"Hi Kweezi, Leek." She beamed. "Glad you could come to P.S. Parents." She studied her bank of screens. "Of course, the three sets you selected are waiting. I'm sure you'll find them more than adequate. If you look at the panel, we'll begin shortly."

The computer registered their retinal patterns and credited their monetary clearinghouse account. The receptionist smiled widely and stood. "Please follow me."

She led them down a long, cheerful hallway. Pictures of beaming children with their chosen parents adorned the wall. To Leek, the portraits were nothing less than meticulous farces. He couldn't help wondering how long the smiling lasted, probably slightly longer than the camera flash used to light the picture.

The receptionist opened a door with "Visiting Room" emblazoned on its front. Pale blue walls, white ceiling tile, and gray, low-pile carpet greeted their eyes. Screens with abstract animation danced on the walls. A large, simulated oak conference table surrounded by comfortable chairs was meant to provide a barrier between the children and their prospective parents. She offered them seats at the table and stepped to the bar in the alcove.

"May I interest you in a beverage?" she asked.

"A beer, please," Leek said. *How refreshing to find an organization with social graces,* he thought.

"Make that two," Kweezi said.

"We have stronger drinks if you'd prefer."

"We'd better not," Kweezi said. "Leek can't hold his liquor, and this decision is too important."

"Of course." The receptionist set two frothy mugs in front of them.

A short man entered the room, and the receptionist introduced him. "This is Roland, your facilitator."

They exchanged the customary greetings and sat. Roland waddled over to the shelf near the bar and selected a large, black binder. Leek wondered why Roland didn't display the information on one of the screens strategically placed around the room. Perhaps tradition outweighed convenience in social situations. Leek possessed little experience with such meetings.

"I'm sure you're familiar with our promotional literature and have familiarized yourselves with our interview process," the man said. "Nevertheless, I'd like to review it so you're in a position to make an educated decision. An assessment of this magnitude needs careful consideration to prevent you from making a poor selection. After all, it is your future."

He waited for their acknowledgment. They nodded.

Roland continued, "We'll give you a half hour to interview each parental set. You may ask them whatever you like. I'll be over there," he pointed to the corner of the room, "to ensure that the prospects don't infringe on your rights. We at P.S. Parents take great pains to screen only the best applicants, but, occasionally, an inadequate set slips through. If you're certain the set you're interviewing isn't appropriate, you may terminate the interview and move onto the next. We don't want you to feel uncomfortable in any way. Once the three interviews are complete, we'll forward the transcripts to your account so you may review it at home. We only require that you make your decision within seventy-two hours. If none of the three are acceptable, we'll provide you with further candidates. Any questions?"

They each shook their head. This was not their first time choosing parents.

Roland pressed a dark blue button on the side of the wall

and the receptionist ushered in two men, each wearing strained grins and explosive eyes. Roland introduced the tall one, whom Leek estimated to be just above six feet tall, as Hayden. He was on the thin side, but not exceptionally lanky, and sported a traditional military flat top. Jordan was a smaller gentleman and overweight. His diminutive ears jutted almost directly away from his head while his fleshy lips were white from the tension in his smile. They sat stiffly in the chairs offered them by Roland. Hayden bounced slightly as his backside hit the chair.

"You may proceed," Roland informed Kweezi and Leek, ignoring the two men.

Leek instinctively referred to Kweezi to ask the first question. It was an unnecessary consideration because she had already begun. "Why do you want to be parents?"

Jordan somehow smiled wider than it seemed possible, and the crow's feet dug more fiercely into his temples.

"We want to give back to society," he said innocently, although a bit static and rehearsed. "We love children and with the shortage of parents today, we thought we'd help out."

Jordan put his hand on Hayden's, who ran his other hand through his upright hair. The motion struck Leek as an attempt to simulate a plane landing on a runway. It was a nervous habit that he knew Kweezi would find maddening. She was O.C.D. about some things, and he knew it would eventually drive her crazy. That simple act might be enough to eliminate this set entirely. Nevertheless, he remained silent as she asked the next question.

"You've seen our bios. Why do you want to be our parents?"

"You like many of the things we do. We thought it would be fun to share experiences, like concerts and...and...stuff, with you?"

Hayden shot him a quick, disquieting gaze. Jordan noticeably shifted in his seat, possibly aware of the implications of his statement. His eyes danced between Kweezi and Leek.

"Of course," Jordan added, "we would only accompany you if you wanted us along. We know children are human beings and can decide if they want parental company."

Leek saw a smirk forming on Kweezi's lips. The interview had suddenly become a game to her, and she drew more satisfaction as the discomfort of her opponents increased.

"What are some of the things you like to do?" Leek interjected before Kweezi completely ruined the interview. He had no intention of playing her game. His goal was to find good parents, not see how much they squirmed under pressure. Kweezi took a swig of beer from her mug and flopped back against the chair. She wiped the foam from her upper lip with a loose sleeve.

"We like the social nets," Jordan offered. "We visit the virtual zoos and museums, read the classics, watch the netcasts, and just hang out."

Silence greeted the answer. Apparently, Hayden took the silence to mean the answer was inadequate. "We also like to visit the sites with new theatrical productions on our HHD unit."

Leek interpreted their response as routine behavior of normal people, although he knew Kweezi would consider the HHD a bribe. Few people owned a holographic high definition screen. The new technology could project a three dimensional image with startling clarity in the center of the room with only a small implant. It was expensive to retrofit HHD from traditional 3-D projection units. Cost, along with short supply, had turned HHD into a new status symbol.

Hayden landed more airplanes on his hair during the silence.

"How long do you expect our relationship to last?" Kweezi challenged.

It was a loaded question that struck Leek as entirely unfair. If they said "forever," it would be an obvious lie since almost no parents lasted longer than four years. If they answered truthfully, it would make them seem unable to make a long term commitment. He almost asked Kweezi to rescind the question but thought better of it. Kweezi had a reason for everything.

"That would be entirely up to the two of you," Jordan replied with a nervous laugh. "We will do whatever we can to be the best parents you ever had and will do our best to meet your needs for as long as you're willing to be with us."

Leek smiled. He was good. Kweezi, apparently satisfied with the clever response as well, continued down a less argumentative path. She asked about their home, their dedication to children, living standards, and what they expected from Kweezi and Leek. The interview finished uneventfully.

Roland allowed a few minutes for Kweezi and Leek to gather their thoughts and then pressed the button on the wall. Two women and one man followed the receptionist to their seats.

Roland stood. "Let me introduce Joanes, Gail, and Brin. You'll have thirty minutes just as before. Please begin."

Leek was not certain he wanted to live in a family with three adults, not that a family with three adults was unordinary. Trinks—triple income, no kids—were the fastest growing segment of society. Families with three adults and one or two children were also becoming more commonplace. The arrangement had its inherent advantages. Two adults could work while the third entertained the kids and administered the house. Triple parent families offered the best stability—most stayed together nearly five years. When one partner wanted a divorce, the other two typically stayed together to offer a constant environment for the children.

During their research, they learned that Gail would stay home with Kweezi and Leek while the other two worked. Gail had been an elementary school teacher until a few years ago, when the new Congress passed laws forcing her to teach more of the "basics" instead of important living skills that taught children how to live in an ever-more complex society. Although she had quit teaching for the right reason, Kweezi felt she might want children for her own to compensate for the loss of her teaching career.

"What would you teach us?" Kweezi asked.

In her less-than-subtle way, she had laid their biggest issue out on the figurative table. Leek could understand her concern. She had been close to their friend Trent through his latest divorce. His mother had attempted to teach him every day, despite the laws against it. Finland had been the first country to outlaw homeschooling on the premise that parents were attempting to instill discriminatory ideas into their children. His mother made him work on lessons almost two hours every day. It didn't take long to receive a divorce, but the experience left him emotionally unbalanced for months afterward. Therapy finally taught him how to accept the pain and deal more appropriately with the trauma. Kweezi didn't want to go through the same experience. Apart from that threat, the family seemed to be an otherwise perfect prospect, which was why they had chosen to interview them.

"I wouldn't teach," Gail answered in a studied tone. "If you were to have a question about something, I'd use my background to show you where to discover the answer for yourselves, but I wouldn't presume to 'teach' you." She twisted her wedding rings around the third finger on each hand. Leek wondered if she were simply nervous or if she were hiding something.

"You must regret that you no longer teach," Kweezi probed, although she attempted to sound virtuous.

Joanes nodded to Kweezi slowly and authoritatively. Brin retained his inexpressive poker face. Presumably, the three had predicted that Gail's past profession might create a problem and created a united front.

"Of course, I miss it," Gail said. "But I have my principles. As a teacher, I didn't want to teach children something that would be harmful to them. It is the same principle that would prevent me from doing the same as a parent. It's against the law and demeans the child as well."

Leek could tell they had extensively prepared as they answered further questions with equal deftness. Despite Kweezi's passion for cross-examination, Leek surmised they wouldn't receive any further useful insights.

Roland called in the third set of parents. The man and woman were like any other pair you'd see at a party. Not only that, but they were two of the most polite adults Leek had ever met with the "Yes, Ma'am" and "No, Sir" and eager, listening eyes. They oozed sincerity all over.

How did they pass P.S. Parents' screening?! Leek thought.

Kweezi's probing questions brought the most intelligible and expressive answers they had ever heard. These jeweled-tongued frauds were amazing, but their deception was obvious. Their beliefs in children's rights were dead giveaways. No adult supported all the children's rights causes. Everyone discriminated in some manner; it was human nature. Rights were mutually exclusive. If you granted one group a right, another group lost a proportional piece of theirs. The goal for government was to balance the rights so that every human being possessed equal shares. Apparently, this parental set didn't seem to understand this most basic concept.

The only thing Leek couldn't understand was their agenda. Could it be money? After all, the government subsidy for children was extremely generous. However, if the parents spent the money on anything other than the children, it would constitute grounds for divorce and criminal retribution. And the subsidy certainly did not compensate for the enormous penalty resulting from mistreating children if that was their intention.

This parental set said they naturally "loved" children and "accepted them for who they are." The interview lasted less than ten minutes. Kweezi and Leek were as convinced as they could be. Roland closed the door behind the hucksters. Their decision would come down to the first two sets only.

Roland provided an oral synopsis of the interviews and expectations. Kweezi and Leek thanked him and left.

The crisp, fall air greeted them as they stood on the sidewalk. Leek thought perhaps the long walk home would clear their minds.

"You know what I'm wondering?" Kweezi asked.

"It's hard to say about you," Leek said, deadpan.

"What if adults want to become parents for the money? Although they can't spend it on themselves, they still reap the benefits of free food and living expenses."

They dead-ended into the Apple Tower, where High and

Broad streets once intersected. They backtracked two blocks.

"I've never met any adult who seemed genuinely concerned for kids," she continued. "I think their 'love' centers around manipulation and power. I simply don't understand why someone would want to control another human being. If only parents could show children the mutual respect they deserve..." Kweezi fell silent. She was back on her soapbox with nothing original left to say.

After several minutes of walking in silence, Leek asked, "So who do you want for our new parents?" He was careful not to encourage another outpouring of contempt on parenting.

"You know what?" She paused briefly but did not wait for an answer, "I don't want any of them."

The statement stopped Leek cold. The two years spent researching agencies and reviewing parental resumes would have been for nothing. "You want to start over?"

"Not at all." A broad smile crossed Kweezi's mouth. "I don't want any parents. Period."

Leek was dumbstruck. Despite being a bit of an insurgent, she always had one foot grounded in realism.

"But we need...," Leek said, "we have to..."

"What do we need? Parents? Why?"

"Because..."

"Because it's the law?"

Leek nodded, but knew there were probably other reasons he could find if he thought about it.

"It's a law that's been held over from a more discriminatory time. What if no one had considered it in the context of our new society? All things must be questioned and compared within our current social context, you know. You've seen what a great life we've had together, and it hasn't been because of our parents. It's been because of what we've had together. Imagine what it would have been like if we'd grown up a mere twenty years ago? We'd have been miserable, slaves to adults whose only desire was to control children and to pick on those smaller than themselves. We wouldn't have had the opportunity to be sibs."

Her statement cut through the dense fog in Leek's mind. It

was a solid argument. They certainly wouldn't have enjoyed the same freedom since it had been a mere fifteen years since the government had granted children the legal right to choose their own siblings. It had worked out beautifully for society.

Still, Leek's doubts persisted. "But everyone has to have parents."

"Why?"

"You need a mother and a father for conception. So, it seems logical the roles would play out through adulthood."

"Logical? Science can emulate the building blocks of a father and a mother. Thankfully, artificial wombs free women from the nine months of inhuman suffering. As for fathers...," she laughed, "their role has been extinct for decades!"

"What about the nurturing of babies? They're entirely helpless and require constant supervision."

"A professional nanny is more efficient than consuming the lives of two adults."

"You're not thinking what I think you're thinking, are you?" Leek asked.

"I am!" Kweezi could barely contain her enthusiasm. "Let's change the law. Parents are irrelevant. Children can do everything we need to survive, especially at our age. Why shouldn't we get the government subsidy ourselves? We could live on our own and spend the money more sensibly. It sure wouldn't be wasted on adults. We've been living without parents for almost two years now. Haven't we had the best time of our lives?"

She was right. They had.

"But what about role models? What about comforting us when we're sick or afraid? It wouldn't be the same without them."

"You're absolutely right, it wouldn't be the same. It would be much better. We have each other for comforting. Our friends and others we meet in the Internet communities provide us with more than we need for guidance. How many adults do you know who have the same sophistication we have?"

Leek could only stare at her beaming face. He had no

rebuttal. He recalled the many happy times with his birth parents and felt the sudden sting of regret as he remembered the divorce. His friend, Joseph, a social worker, had helped him through the difficult times that followed and taught him how to deal with the pain. His birth parents weren't bad people, nor were they bad parents. Kweezi would never understand; it was impossible to change her mind once it was made up. She felt none of the remorse and had no need for counseling when she divorced her own birth parents. She had shed no tear for either of their parental divorces.

Leek had seen her in this mood before. Kweezi always wanted to change the world. She'd explain the situation to the children's rights political action committees on the Internet. Once she described her vision of a world that could be, they'd dedicate themselves to her cause, and it would easily become a major issue during the next election. The timing was advantageous politically; a backlash was simmering against the new Congress and its shift to the radical right. Many P.A.C.s were searching for a unifying issue to rally behind in order to move the country back to more moderate ground. This would be the one; Kweezi would make sure of it. He trusted her as many others already did and would.

Leek smiled, matching Kweezi's infectious grin. They walked with renewed fire in their bellies. Shortly, they passed the straggly man they'd seen earlier. They didn't stop. They were focused on the world that could be, not the inferior world that had been.

Maybe there was something to do in Columbus after all.

Andrew Miller

Andrew is a proclaimed Jack-of-all-trades—though he may not be the one to proclaim it. Mechanic, carpenter, tech support, community organizer, all terms that have been used to describe Andrew, a list that now includes "fiction author."

"Broken" is Andrew's first recognized foray into short stories, an art he has come to love and produce regularly. His stories are culled from a life lived on the edges of American culture.

In 2012, Andrew plans to attend Otterbein University to hone his craft as a creative writer. In his spare time from working for the State of Ohio, Andrew is currently a freelance journalist for a number of local news organizations, such as WOSU, *ThisWeek Community Newspapers* and *Columbus CEO*.

He loves playing with his daughter, Sophie, making up adventures on his World War 2-esque Ural sidecar motorbike. You'll see him sun or snow, traversing the streets of Columbus. Motorbike or bicycle, he believes two wheels are always better than four.

Andrew lives with Sophie, two cats and his partner, Gail, in their Upper Arlington home, which suffers from a constant state of remodel, thanks to Andrew being that Jack-of-all-trades.

BROKEN

By Andrew Miller

"Let's get out of here."

Jackson tugged at Lisa's arm, sweat running down the side of his face, both of them moist from the stale, humid air.

"No, I'm staying. Knuckles Lee's up next!" Lisa shouted over the thrashing sound of drums, bass and guitar, which assaulted the audience, making conversation nearly impossible.

"I gotta go. I can't stand the crowd anymore."

Sweating bodies moved against each other, less in harmony than struggle, the sound launching itself from the wall of speakers like an attack.

"What?"

"Gotta go! See you at home."

"What?"

"Yeah. Okay, see you."

Jackson didn't bother shouting this time; instead he used his sarcastic sweet voice and kissed her cheek, his lips barely contacting her skin, his disconnected embrace echoed by her body, sloping away from him like a tree split by lightning. Throughout the brief, uncomfortable exchange, Lisa's gaze was focused on the eyes of another man standing near the stage who was looking back at her, undeterred by the sonic blasts.

Crowds at Columbus's Bend Bar weren't known for their friendly demeanor. So many corn-fed, farm-raised punk rockers meant Jackson had to push aggressively past the stage area, the sound booth, and along the length of the 1800s-era, hand-carved maple bar. Surprisingly, it wasn't wholly out of place. Covered in booze, as its craftsman intended, but now no longer surrounded by Victorian décor. Instead it hid behind punk rock concert posters and a floor-to-ceiling mural of Kurt Cobain, shotgun in one hand, slumped over, relieved of all his brain matter, the ghosts of Hunter S. Thompson and Hemingway splattered behind him.

"F' this place," Jackson muttered, punching open the barroom door, letting it swing closed behind him on the sticky summer night.

I'm sick of this scene, of this life, he thought.

A year ago, Jackson was doing the same thing, thinking these same thoughts. Back then a brief flash of inspiration found him at Art's Art on High, buying a sketchpad, some paints and brushes.

Where's that sketchpad now? Sitting blank, in that damn cubicle, doing nothing useful, like me. The tempo of his thoughts kept rising.

Pills and thrills won't pay my bills—after my Uncle Sam-bam beats me, it makes me want to kill, Kill, KILL... The lyrics of the song ran through Jackson's head as he walked away from the Bend.

Musicians. They spend their days creating something new, something all their own.

But Jackson knew he wasn't creating anything—he was self-destructing.

"And what am I doing, huh? What am I doing? Making misery! I'm just miserable." His words echoed off grate-covered windows and graffitied walls.

Jackson swore he'd never be like his old man, an aging jock with nothing but "the good old days." But right out of high school, Jackson fell into a bottle just like his dad, and now, when he found himself hunkered down at the bar, all that was left to talk about were his own glory days.

Instead of the gridiron though, it was that lithograph he'd made in grade school that was included in a National Art Education pamphlet or the poem that was accepted into an all high school literary journal.

Lisa expected Jackson would leave ahead of her, as he almost always did. He told her once that by leaving early he was a little bit better than her, than everyone in that bar. Of

116

BROKEN • *Andrew Miller*

course it wasn't true and Lisa knew it. She didn't believe
Jackson was any different—and certainly not better—than her.
They were both drunks regardless of who left the bar first. She
was sure he couldn't change, and she didn't want to change.
Lisa liked her life, or at least felt comfortable in its consistency,
and tonight she knew she wanted to salvage her evening.

The man in progressive eye contact with Lisa popped
another Adderall and watched Jackson exit the bar.

"Joey," he yelled. "I'll be back!"

He made his way through the mass of bodies to Lisa. She
grabbed his hand and led him past the "Employees Only" sign,
down to the basement of the Bend.

"Is it cool if we're down here, anyone going to give us shit
about it?" he asked.

"What's your name?"

Lisa already knew the answer, but, as a veteran of many
brief encounters, she didn't like to hint at any sort of long-term
attraction.

"Brian. You're Lisa, right?"

He answered a little too quickly, the multiple doses of
speed he'd taken causing his reactions to be out of sync, his
thoughts a little warped.

"Lisa, right. Don't worry about remembering it."

Brian, not recognizing this statement for what it was,
bragged, "I won't, but you'll remember me."

"Sure thing, Handsome."

She wasn't an employee anymore, but she had been. More
importantly, she'd made this same trip with various members
of the bar staff on other occasions. They all knew the score and
turned a blind eye to her escapades.

"Don't worry about the door. If anyone comes down, it
won't be anything they haven't seen before," she said coolly.

Brian's retort, which sounded sexy and voracious to his
own ears, was as ham-fisted as his attempts to undress her: "I
want to tear you apart and devour you." He fumbled with Lisa's

clothes, grabbing at her awkwardly, forcefully kissing her.

"Calm down, Tiger," Lisa said, kissing much more deliberately, licking his neck and pulling at his clothes. Meeting Brian's childish comments, she played along. "I'm the hunter tonight. I'm in control. You're my trophy…I'm not your girl…"

Brian remained oblivious to Lisa's intentions even as she whispered to him, "You're my possession, and when I'm done with you, I'm going to throw you away."

Tonight, though, as with most nights, Lisa's hunt for a physical release wouldn't satisfy her deeper desire for emotional attraction. The last time she felt emotionally attracted to anyone was Jackson. Before Jackson there was a boy in high school and another during her brief stint at university. All three attempts at a regular, committed relationship had turned into messy webs of miscommunication and mistrust.

Three strikes and you're out, she had thought. She no longer trusted attachment, at least not beyond Jackson's service as life support.

Brian focused on the task at hand, interested only in his own masculine power, while Lisa's thoughts floated in and out, her mind racing to the complexities of her relationship with Jackson, then back to the physical pleasure of the here and now. Back and forth during the encounter it was as if she and Brian weren't even occupying the same world, much less one another's skin.

Of course I'll go home tonight, she thought. She always did. *Where else would I go?*

There was a sense of security in the third floor walk-up that she and Jackson shared, and she couldn't bear to let go of it. Theirs wasn't always a happy existence, but she accepted that even misery loves company. Lisa believed she still loved Jackson, at least sort of, imagining his body as hers quivered next to Brian's. Her brain struggled against her desires, her emotions trapped in between.

118

Only blocks away, Jackson drowned himself in self-loathing and another good drunk, a perfect circle of depression that on most nights medicated him to sleep. He walked slightly cocked to one side, stumbling and tripping on occasional cracks in the pavement, weaving in and out of consciousness. Pairs of lights from cars and buses illuminated his path. Occasional strangers passed by him.

"Hey," he'd say to them, blankly.

He thought about the fact that no one ever responded. Except for the time he got mugged, when the response was a gun, or maybe he'd been tricked, maybe it was just a length of pipe that felt like a gun in his back. Still, he persisted.

How do I always end up here? he wondered.

Stumbling along, he imagined yet another morning. The alarm screaming in his ear and destroying his dehydrated, snoring slumber, bringing him back to the reality of work, of paying his and Lisa's bills. Of hating his job, his life. He imagined all the times he'd said, "Never again," but hadn't meant it.

In fact, he was already planning for a drunken outing next weekend—another bar, another band, the same boring conversations with his friends. Another lonely night passed out at home, waking up with Lisa next to him, curled up inches away from her, yet millions of miles away from her affection.

Rounding the last corner onto Neil Avenue, just blocks from home, Jackson stepped off the curb onto the remnants of a discarded beer bottle, sending him tumbling to the ground.

"Dammit!"

He cried out in pain, his ankle throbbing and shards of glass in his hands. When he tried to stand, he couldn't. His body prone on the street, he picked the glass out of one hand while wincing at the shards in the other.

Lisa will be by soon enough, or someone will, he thought. *I'll just wait. If I have to, I'll sleep it off out here. Hell, this wouldn't be the first time.*

His ankle was shattered. Between the alcohol and adrenaline he felt less pain than he should, but he still couldn't stand. There was no way he would get home under his own power.

"I guess it's you and me, Mr. Light Pole," Jackson mumbled as he leaned against it, his head slumping down, a subtle snore escaping his throat, the air around him thick with his own stench of alcohol and cigarettes.

As the music pulsed from above, Lisa and Brian's bodies, sweaty skin on sweaty skin, pulsed together, too. The basement was just below the dance floor, and in the old, overcrowded building the joists were visibly heaving, like the lovers' chests.

Brian broke first, his tension released, screaming "Jesus Christ!" before falling into Lisa, who had enjoyed herself too, but, so trapped in her thoughts, couldn't be fully in the moment and satisfied. Her hands against Brian's chest, she pushed him away from her easily, as he attempted a kiss.

"I'm not your girlfriend," she declared. "Thanks, little man. You give better eye then you do action."

Lisa's cold dismissal caught Brian off guard, and his defense was limp at best.

"Nice. No wonder your boy left."

Lisa knew she'd hit her target.

For Lisa, this was almost always her response, regardless of the outcome. Deflating her lovers immediately after intimacy kept them from nurturing any attachment. She thought of herself as the clichéd black widow. She even sported the tattoo of one just above her panty line, on her right hip, an irony that seemed to escape Jackson.

Brian shook himself clean, pulled his clothes back into place and muttered, "Skank," as he slunk back upstairs.

Lisa knew he'd say something even if she didn't actually hear it, so she preemptively yelled, "Don't come back for more, you little string-bean!" before the deafening blast of rock-n-roll invaded the basement as Brian left.

With the door slammed shut, the volume again halved, Lisa's hunt was over and she felt disconnected from the jungle above. Taking her time, she used the filthy, stained utility sink in the corner to wash up.

"Just another day at the office," she thought aloud.

Fragments of a mirror remained above the sink from another night, when another drunken hook-up pitched a beer bottle at Lisa in a fit of rage. She watched her cracked reflection, and wondered what she'd expected from all of this.

Brian wouldn't notice until later that Lisa relieved him of ten bucks while she disrobed him. It wasn't enough to make her feel it was real thievery, but it was enough to give her a rush of excitement—a feat of daring that she felt deserved rewarded.

"Hmm, I think this calls for a vodka tonic, in a big-girl glass," Lisa said, clicking closed the cap of her vamp-red lipstick, walking past the boxes, broken chairs and beer-bottle crates and back up the stairs.

Filled to the brim with booze and amphetamines, Brian had satisfied his desire to get off with Lisa, but she'd left him bitter and vengeful.

"Hey, Joey," he yelled at his friend. "I'm feelin' good. Let's get out of here and tear it up somewhere else."

Brian was thin but not weak, with short, clean-cut hair and waffle-making, shit-kicker boots courtesy of the U.S. Army. Back from a tour in the 'Stan, he was looking for a good time, which didn't always equate to what civilian society considered acceptable.

"Lead the way." Joey idolized Brian and was always game for anything he had in mind.

Pushing through the crowd, Brian elbowed heads and punched guts, letting his adrenaline feed his aggression, and vice versa. Joey lurched behind, much less physically aggressive than Brian, but happy to throw a punch when Brian was looking.

Outside the bar, the explosive sound faded behind them.

"How was that chick?"

"Look man, she wanted it bad. Guess her little boyfriend just isn't man enough."

Joey was rarely the one chosen by girls, and his lack of experience only exacerbated his immaturity.

"I bet you rocked her. Who's her boyfriend anyhow, isn't it that loser Jackson? That dude talks too much, always has some idea but then he's always there, sittin' at the bar, talkin' shit and not doin' shit. Stupid asshole. Probably doesn't even know she's gettin' it from a real man." Joey's mouth ran on, as it often did, without realizing that Brian wasn't listening. "That guy thinks he's got some big plan, but he doesn't have shit. We should let him know."

"Yep," Brian said. "Somebody needs to give him the message."

Brian couldn't get Lisa's words out of his head. "Better eye than action" and "little string bean." He thought, *fuck her, and Jackson, he sure as hell can't be worth more than what I just gave her.*

Little did he know Jackson would have agreed with him, and with Joey. Jackson wasn't the one for Lisa, and he let himself down regularly by talking about a life he was afraid to live.

Joey egged Brian on. "You should kick his ass out of the picture. Take what's yours."

Within minutes, Joey and Brian reached Neil Avenue, and spied Jackson on the corner. Brian saw his opportunity to unload his hurt and anger in the only way he knew how—with violence.

"I think my boots are a little too clean, what 'bout you, Joey?"

"Let's break them in!" Joey squealed, knowing a bit of aggro was imminent and excited to see his idol in action.

Their pace quickened and became more deliberate, like a double-time march into the front line of battle, their target oblivious to the coming attack.

Brian never broke stride. He used his momentum to land a punishing blow to Jackson's limp torso, connecting his steel-toed boot to Jackson's ribcage, halfway up the side of his body, snapping two ribs in one motion, and knocking Jackson over, face down in the street.

Joey followed this up by launching himself into the air, landing the soles of his boots on Jackson's back, sending the shattered edge of one of his ribs through his left lung.

In a brief moment of consciousness, Jackson rolled to the side and spit the blood from his mouth. Staring upward, the streetlight now appeared as bright as the sun, out of focus and blinding, a star falling into him.

Joey looked down; Jackson's ankle twisted unnaturally, and now, blood rose from his chest, forming a puddle in his mouth.

"Damn Brian, nice one! Let's get out of here before he sobers up." Joey pulled at Brian's shoulders, nervously laughing, no longer excited, instead anxious and ready to run.

Brian looked down into Jackson's vacant eyes. He knew he'd gone too far this time—this was irreparable damage. He'd seen this look before in battle. But this wasn't Afghanistan. Someone would care, probably even Lisa.

The streetlight flickered, a pair of headlights turned onto the street a few blocks down, and Brian looked up for a moment.

We're all broken, all of us, he thought, before fleeing into the dark night.

Justin Nicholas Hanson

Justin N. Hanson, twenty-two, was born and raised in Columbus, Ohio; he also spent much time in New York City, which he considers a second home.

Justin recently graduated with distinction from The Ohio State University, where he studied English and writing under such local literary titans as Manuel Luis Martinez, Lee. K Abbott, and critic James Phelan.

"Old, Young Men" is Hanson's first published story, drawing its scenery and characters from his eclectic Columbus upbringing. He believes that literature should both entertain and instruct, and he insists that art matters, and not just for art's sake.

As a writer, Justin is a realist, constructing tales based on the extraordinary problems of ordinary human beings. Justin lives downtown and enjoys frequenting the main library, dining in German Village, and trading drinks and stories in the Short North with friends, fellow writers, and artists of Columbus.

He plans to pursue a Masters, M.F.A, or PhD in the near future. Justin hopes you enjoy his story of Columbus, and you find within it something worthwhile.

Readers can email Justin at jnhanson.75@gmail.com.

OLD, YOUNG MEN
By Justin Nicholas Hanson

I remember when I was twenty-one and leaving college
that I wanted desperately to decide something about life. That
endless question of youth—"Who am I?"— terrified me, Danny
Marcum, the poor kid from the east side, surrounded and
mocked by the wealth and comfort of others. I knew that some
men had it all, that they possessed some secret to prosperity, and
all my young life I aimed to learn it.

One night in October 2009 when the recession strangled
all of America, my best friend Vinny interrupted my lonesome
thoughts when he pulled outside my apartment in his brand
new Cadillac. Vinny's father, Big Frank the slumlord, had
summoned us to dinner, an old man's habit to keep in touch with
the next generation. And it was on that frozen night that my
life's pendulum swung, leading me on the road to the man I am
today.

"Hey, Danny," Vinny called. "Come on out, asshole, and
see the new wheels."

I lumbered out of my east side apartment to survey Vinny's
prize. The car was magnificent: a 2005 Cadillac CTS with
leather interior, tinted windows, and enough electronic doo-dads
to make Captain Kirk jealous. "I think it even came with pickup
line suggestions," said Vinny, "and when we get lost, it calls
NASA."

We pulled our coats around us under a gray sheet of sky
that clasped Columbus in a grip of cold. We sped out of the
neighborhood, the defroster roaring, drunk on our invincibility
in an automobile whose cost exceeded the down payments of
the houses we passed. Some of the black neighborhood kids
watched us go by. I lived in a black neighborhood. Vinny had
already purchased two homes there, including the one I rented
from him for next to nothing, and he aimed at owning a whole
block by the time he was thirty—textbook slumlord.

"Did you see those little niggers?" he asked. "They went, 'looky there, looky there, there goes da landlord.'" He laughed at his cleverness. It disgusted me, but I winced and forced a laugh, hoping for a change in subject.

"So be honest," he said, "what do you think of the car?"

"You have to ask?" I said. "It's beautiful, a work of art, the Sistine Chapel of automobiles, purrs like a kitten. Angels must be singing about it now."

Vinny smiled and nodded. "I'm going to be rolling in the pussy with this thing. They're gonna have to wait in line."

I rolled my eyes. "Maybe you should get some numbered tickets made. It would be more efficient."

"Nah," said Vinny, "I want to be fair. It'll be first come, first served, or the other way around." He laughed again and lit a cigarette. "Keep riding with me, Danny, and you might get some high-class tail, too."

"Speak for yourself," I said, "I'm doing just fine. Are you going to miss the Mustang?" I asked. It had been his first car; we had grand times in it.

"Not really, it ran its course. Besides," Vinny said, inhaling his cigarette, "the Mustang is a boy's car. This is a man's car."

"I hear that."

"Seriously, when women see this thing, and see the way you and I dress, there won't be much to ponder. They're going to know we have some cash, and that we know how to play the game."

He had a point, I'll give him that. We both realized at an early age that the world had no rules, only games. For Vinny, this was always somehow intuitive and a part of his upbringing. For me, a life of careful observation taught me that certain characteristics divided the haves and have-nots. I knew politically correct language stabilized the naked inequities of the world, favors and kickbacks made during golf outings fueled its commerce, and men grew wealthy suckling from the breast of every bureaucracy. I knew certain things existed only as fairy

126

tales, smoke and mirrors to distract the weak—things like the American Dream and Mega Millions to give some faint hope to the downtrodden.

But I stopped caring at some point; there didn't seem much reason to care when nothing changes. Although we differed in every possible way, Vinny and I shared this cynicism. It drew us together at school. No one else thought or felt like we did, and that made the two of us seem like family. Big Frank could have afforded any private school in the city, but Vinny's old man sent him to a public school, my public school, to "toughen me up, I guess," as Vinny had once told me. That was how we met. We noticed our mutual bitterness immediately, and in the secret torment that aged us beyond our years, misery found company.

Neither of us felt young, and we did our best not to look it. We tried our best to be old-school handsome like Newman and Redford. We wore slacks, buttoned shirts and ties, shaved with safety razors, and styled our generous hair with Brylcreem ("*A little dab'll do ya*"). Our scents were that of men, not some noisome locker room concoction, but Old Spice for me and Aqua Velva for Vinny. We even spoke the way we thought old-timers might: to us, women were "broads," "Ivy Leaguers" were kiss-asses and know-it-alls, and we referred to our matching leather jackets as our "threads." We delighted in trading banter with the old men, who smiled at us when we would say things like, "looks like we're shittin' in high cotton now" to refer to progress, or "about as useful as balls on a priest," for, well, the obvious.

Vinny was average in height and thick, but not in a stocky or disproportionate way. He had blond hair, thick lips, green eyes, and broad shoulders; you wouldn't likely guess that he was Italian until you heard his name—DePassio.

I was the opposite: a hulking six-foot-two inches tall; thick, dark hair; and a face and disposition that the literary types might term Byronic, traits I inherited from my father, the drunkest Irishman in the city, who skipped town about a dozen years and a hundred cocktail waitresses ago. No one we ever met believed we were under thirty. Most people thought it was a joke if and when we told them we were twenty-one years old. It settled in our eyes, I think—that look of knowing, of pains endured and weathered heartache.

"So," said Vinny, "big graduation coming up, college boy."

"That's right," I said.

"I hope it works out for you, Danny boy. When I think of all the time I wasted in college, I can't believe I ever went at all."

"If I only knew then what I know now, as they say—"

"I honestly don't know what the hell people see in it," Vinny said. "I'm twenty-one years old and already I'm making more money than those little idiots will be making in ten years, even with their precious degrees—sixty-thousand dollar pieces of paper if you ask me. Honestly, the only explanation for it is that they're stupid, plain and simple. Well, except for you, Danny."

"As always, thanks for the endorsement." Vinny had a hobby in education-bashing. He had gone to a community college in Baltimore for two years to play lacrosse. I don't recall what he studied there, and, frankly, I doubt he remembered either. Vinny's education took place years before with his father, who groomed him from an early age. His only knowledge, only care, was money. It consumed him.

"I'm serious though, you know the game better than anyone I know, better than I do maybe, which is why it amazes me that you're still thinking about becoming a teacher. Get wise, my friend. Get wise."

"I'm still up in the air," I said.

"Danny," said Vinny, lighting another cigarette, "I know I'm not smart, but I know money, business, and people. I'm going to be a rich man soon, and I have a feeling that one day you're going to be one too. Come on, really, you know that nobody gives a shit about some teacher or professor or whatever.
128

I mean they don't get paid a damn. What, my friend, is the upside?"

"A feeling, I guess."

"What about The Room, buddy?" Vinny said. The Room, as I called it, was my secret fantasy; I had only ever told Vinny about it. "Remind me what The Room is."

"The Room, as you know, is that secret place filled with cigar smoke and guys sipping on Lagavulin scotch," I told him, for what felt like the one-hundredth time.

"And what happens in The Room?" Vinny said, delving into my subconscious.

"In The Room, guys wearing tuxedos rule the world. They make million-dollar deals, get jobs for their friends, and expand their power. They have names like Rockefeller, Morgan, and Kennedy, and nothing is beyond their reach."

Vinny smiled. "And what have you always wanted, Danny boy, ever since you realized you were a poor schmuck living in the shithole where I found you?"

"To be in The Room," I confessed to Vinny, my after-hours priest.

"So do what you have to do—get in The Room. You're smart enough, just do it. We can't keep having this conversation, man; if you don't get wise soon I have the feeling you're going to be lecturing snot-nosed little shits about the Articles of Consideration while I'm on a cruise by my lonesome in the Mediterranean, you dig?"

"Confederation," I said. "And, yeah, I dig."

For a guy whom I suspected was mostly illiterate, Vinny read me like a book. To compensate for my seedy origins, I made my way through high school on my grades, athletics and structured likeability. While Vinny worked on cars and landscaped after school, I studied Latin and Geometry, earning straight A's. I joined the football team to be known as a "scholar athlete," Vinny joined because Big Frank told him to. Even then I was a cynic, and I knew that all my hard work and activities weren't for any genuine desire, but because I was trying to be the Golden Boy.

A few of my teachers took an interest and encouraged me. I looked up to them for their honesty and passion. There was Mr. Geyer with his lectures on Pericles and virtue, Mr. Yanok who read *Hamlet* as well as Burbage or Olivier, and Ms. Osland who was positively giddy with geometrical proofs. Sometimes I imagined myself in front of a classroom, explaining the Battle of Marathon or lonely Miss Havisham in such a way as to pierce through an entire room of teenage apathy. "But there's no money in it," Vinny was always quick to remind me.

When it came time for college, I convinced Ohio State that it was such a miracle that some poor product of the nation's deteriorating education system had managed a 35 on his ACT that I deserved a full ride. I chose Finance as a major ("the future of the country depends on it," a welcoming assistant dean told me like a sanctimonious politician), but thoughts of teaching fueled me. Since the day that letter came and I edged closer and closer toward graduation, the only thing I felt that my major taught me was the cold, pitiless nature of dollars and cents. But, then again, in a nation of glorified accountants, it was as good a degree as any.

"Let's punch it," Vinny said, and the Cadillac motored along the 70 West freeway over Columbus. The city stretched out before us, the buildings loitering in the sky of our dismal Midwestern town, a place caught between a fledgling metropolis and a suburb, an abnormal clash of small town hicks with trendy, liberal hipsters. There were the wealthy people in the North, the provincial country people in the South, the gangs and destitute on the West Side, and the African-American and poor neighborhoods in the East and the outlying suburbs. The town was a mix of the insular and the erudite, a collage of rich and poor, past and future. We looked upon the buildings, the town, with such disdain. In our minds it was still a cow town and the specter of our past, enervator of our youth.

130

"I can't wait to get out of this goddamn town," said Vinny.

"Hear, hear." I said. "You better punch the gas; we don't want to keep Big Frank waiting."

The Cadillac burst to one hundred miles per hour, and the feeble sights of the Columbus interstate zoomed by us as if we had launched to light speed. Vinny dodged effortlessly in and out of traffic, smoking his cigarette with a ghoulish delight as we navigated our way through imminent highway death. It seemed in seconds we had made our exit and cruised south through the barren town. Just past eight o'clock we arrived at our destination: Tommy Flanagan's pub and pizza parlor, an institution of the south side renowned for its beer and specialty pizzas with their mysterious crust—the secret ingredient to which, local rumor had it, was a precise allotment of maple syrup.

Vinny and I approached the bar, loosened our ties and prepared to imbibe. Vinny's old man sat at the bar. Big Frank didn't bother to stand up, but greeted us with a curt "Boys" and shook our hands. Even at sixty-two, Big Frank was still big in every way: he was as broad and thick as a mailbox with hands like bricks; he lived in an immense ranch house out in the country; and, most importantly, he told big stories—tales about football in Texas, yarns about hunting bear in Alaska, odysseys about sailing the Mediterranean in search of the past. He told his stories with the skill of bards and thespians, leaping from his chair to act out certain portions, mimicking the accents of the Greeks and Creoles he had met, and always pausing just before the punch line to arouse the maximum interest. He had long, gray hair and his ruddy face sported a fluffy mustache. He knew Italian from his youth and learned Spanish to communicate to his construction workers. He had voluntarily stopped drinking when he was thirty-five because, as he said, "I had gotten everything out of it I could, been there, done that," so now he only drank ginger ale, a fact that somehow unnerved Vinny.

"Say there, Danny boy," Big Frank said, "how's the

hammer hanging?"

"Short and fat," I replied.

Big Frank always liked me, and I looked up to him. He liked me because I came from nothing but was smart enough to work the system. When I visited Vinny's place during high school, I often spent dinners discussing politics or economics with Frank while Vinny just ate silently, waiting for a mundane subject to arise so he could interject. Unlike the people I usually debated, Big Frank had no politics, no agenda, no particular leanings one way or the other. He lived above the common political, ethical, or moral persuasions. He fascinated me in his inability to be classified. The self-made men I knew believed in determinism, and "nature" over "nurture," and resented the working poor for their laziness, for not slaving for riches like they did. But Big Frank lacked disdain for the working class. He detached himself from such concerns and merely took his place at the top. He seemed to be the keeper of some secret knowledge of life and its workings, but he wasn't the type to orate, write, or philosophize about it.

"What will you have to drink, Danny boy?" asked Big Frank. "Don't tell me you're going to order some piss-tasting beer like the rest of college kids your age."

"Long is the way and dark that leads up from light beer and into scotch," I said.

Frank laughed. "Champagne taste on a beer budget, huh? You better let me pick up the tab, Danny," he said, turning to the bartender. "A nice scotch for the kid, Barry, and your strongest ginger ale for me."

"Scotch for me too," said Vinny, trying to seat himself between me and Big Frank.

The drinks were served quickly; Big Frank had been a regular at Flanagan's for decades. One of the kitchen guys, a skinny white kid, brought the pizza and we dug in. We made small talk as the barroom carnival rotated. There were men who wore jeans, others who wore ties. Some men were shaven, others were scruffy. Some men used obscenities while others spoke genteel. They seemed like species to me, classed and coded by their clothes and diction, displaying their backgrounds and destinies with certain habits and movements. The lower ones drank cheaply, spoke vulgar English, dressed foolishly, and didn't know when to speak or be silent. They rushed with their food and drink, always complained, and never knew their limits. There was the smell of them, my father's smell—the smell of earthy musk, Marlboros, and kerosene if he had been working construction. I was ashamed of that breed because I knew I came from them.

All my life I knew those men, the ones that talked of their football days like it was the Super Bowl, the ones who bitched and moaned about the government or their bosses, the ones who took their breakfast from a forty-ounce bottle and played cards with their kid's lunch money. I was afraid of becoming one of them, afraid that something genetic within me would trap me in the east side of Columbus forever. I wanted something to save me from all that.

"Come over here, Danny," said Big Frank, holding his ginger ale. "Let's talk." Big Frank briskly signaled for Vinny to vacate his seat.

"What's on your mind, Frank?" I said. "Trying to figure out when the next bubble will burst?"

"Smart ass," he said, grinning. "So, Vincent just told me that you're thinking about a change in your future. Thinking of giving up on that idea of teaching then?"

"It's been a thought," I said, shrugging.

"Why's that, Danny?"

I smiled because I knew what Vinny had told him, and I knew that Big Frank had already read my mind. "Well, I'm thinking, Frank, that I'm getting into the wrong game. I think I've had it all wrong lately."

"Really," he said. "How so?"

"It's a lot of things. I know I won't ever be a somebody

as a teacher, doesn't matter where I go or what I do—it's just a meager existence, and I want more."

Big Frank nodded without looking at me. "What *don't* you want, son?"

"I don't want to be a cog in a wheel," I said.

"Do you have any other ideas?"

I swirled the whiskey around in my glass, as though trying to decipher some murky wisdom in the iodine liquid. "A few ideas, none outstanding. Developed investment stuff or law; I don't know though. I can't seem to figure things out..."

Frank nodded, gulped down his ginger ale, announced "two more," and looked at me solemnly.

"So," Frank said, "you can't decide if you want to be an honest man or a crook."

We laughed.

"Come on, Danny. You were never meant to stand in front of a blackboard and holler at students. You're too smart. I knew we would have this talk one day," Frank said, smiling with excitement. "You did good, kid, real good. I couldn't imagine getting those scholarships and all the way you did, but you did it and here you are a couple of months from a college degree and the world on your fingertips." Big Frank drew me closer, as though about to whisper.

"Hey, Frank," said Vinny, looking up from his pizza. "Let's go outside so I can show you the Caddy."

Big Frank agreed, saying he would allow his son to indulge him with a cigarette out in the night air. The three of us left the tavern. Everyone lit up but me, and we walked over to admire Vinny's ride.

"Now that's a sharp car," said Big Frank. "Reminds me of the 1975 Cadillac Seville I bought right off the line, a beautiful car and worth the money I spent on it; and to think, everyone told me to get a Mercedes. Not bad, Vincent, not bad."

Vinny beamed. "Yeah, this is a man's car, isn't it, Frank? I had to get rid of the Mustang; it was just too childish. Besides, a

134

landlord needs a landlord car," Vinny said, laughing.

We turned away from Vinny's prize and walked back towards the bar. As we walked, I noticed a skinny white kid with furtive eyes heading out to the parking lot, and recognized him as one of the dishwashers. He had a buzzed hair cut, a bony face, and the gaunt appearance of a corpse—a classic drug addict. I thought about what Freud had said: *Biology is destiny*. He paced through the parking lot with his head towards the ground and entered a vehicle at the far end of the lot. Although the car was unlit, we could tell there were other people inside.

"Well, well," said Big Frank, "looks like Tommy's parking lot is also the local drug emporium. Not at our place." Big Frank turned to Vinny, "I'm going inside to let Tommy know he's hired an addict for a busboy. You two do the honors of giving him his walking papers." With that, Big Frank walked back into Flanagan's, leaving Vinny and me outside.

Two minutes later the dishwasher exited the car and headed back toward the restaurant. Another man got out as well, hands in his pockets and head pointed towards the ground as he walked off down the street. Just as the dishwasher was about to re-enter the bar, Vinny stepped in his path.

"Was it a good deal?"

"What are you talking about, man?"

"I heard meth is in short supply right now," Vinny said, still standing in the dish man's path, "so it must have been a good deal. Or was it crack? Crack is always good money."

"Man, I don't know what you're talking about," said the dishwasher. He looked around the parking lot and back toward the bar door before settling his eyes back on Vinny.

"Look," he said, "I've got to get back to work."

"No, you're done working here. Trust me. But it looks like you've got a nice enterprise to fall back on," Vinny said, his voice rising. I felt nervous, not because of the kid but because I knew Vinny expected something of me—Big Frank, too. I knew I had to do something.

"Whatever, man. I'm not into that shit. My girlfriend waits for me during my shift, so I stepped out to see her."

I saw my opportunity and issued a high, false laugh. "Your girlfriend waits for you during your shift?" I said. "What's she got, separation anxiety?"

"Whatever, I'm going back to work," said the dishwasher as he tried to brush by Vinny. Vinny hit him square and clean in the nose. He hit him with none of the skill or dexterity of a boxer, just brute, concentrated power. The dishwasher dropped like a weight, holding his hands to his face as blood rushed out like tap water. *Vae Victis*, I thought, for this kid and other kids like him.

I watched him writhing on the ground, trying to push himself up with his skeletal fingers. I couldn't see Vinny, but I could feel him watching me, and sense his judgment. My legs inched my body forward. The world seemed to slow down: sound receded, the cold air lost its bite, and my breathing halted. The kid stood up and I decked him again. He fell down, sputtering, and I saw Vinny's sharp smile, felt the ice in his sneer.

Vinny knelt down and blew smoke in his face, grabbing him by the throat. "You're done," Vinny said, his eyes glowing. "Consider that deal your severance pay. If you walk into that building again, I'll have the police on your ass and you can go back to the pen where you belong, you drug-addict piece of shit. Todd Hunter, Mackey, Fuller—all cops I know."

The kid choked on blood. "What did I do?" he whispered. His eyes pleaded with Vinny for an answer.

"You're not cut out for this place," Vinny said. "Go back where you belong, kid. Go back to nowhere." The dishwasher got up and walked into the back alley.

Vinny turned to me and smiled, "Let's go. I feel like a Guinness."

We went back inside the bar. My head was swimming. We joined Big Frank. Vinny gave his father a look, and Frank gave
136

him the slightest of nods. "Come on over here, Danny," said Big Frank, "let's keep talking."

I walked over, ordered a beer, and sat down with Frank. It was as though nothing had just happened. "Let me tell you a little story, Danny," Frank said, sipping his ginger ale, "about when I was your and Vinny's age, and maybe you'll be able to get some insight on your current situation."

"I'm all ears."

"I got into construction and real estate when I was about twenty-three," said Big Frank. "By the time I was twenty-nine, I had sixty properties around Columbus and I was rolling in $13,000 a month, and that was back in the seventies. I bought a losing construction company and was able to turn it around. I cut down on labor and materials so I could underbid any roofing contractor in the city. So when I was in my twenties, my friends and I just lived. You would never find us at home on a Friday or Saturday night; we were always at some restaurant, dance club, or pool hall, living the life or picking up women."

"Like *The Hustler,* huh Frank?" Vinny butted in. Frank ignored him and continued.

"See, we never sat around and watched T.V. or played video games like the little jackasses today," said Big Frank. "If it wasn't making us money or getting us laid, we wouldn't waste our time. And we had no problem with women—it works out when you have means. We'd show up to the club on a Saturday night always dressed to the nines. We'd wear suits and ties, our shirt collars would be stiff as cardboard from all the starch we ordered in them and our shoes looked like mirrors after we spit-shined them with cotton balls. One month when I was twenty-six, I set the record," said Frank, smiling and finishing his drink. "Seventeen different women in seventeen days." Vinny beamed behind his father.

The restaurant was emptying behind us. Dozens of suits and ties, jeans and plaid shirts blended together on their way out the door. I was shocked to see some of them embracing, laughing, talking with each other, and patting backs like old friends.

"But my point is you and Vincent sit around too damn much, especially living in a hayseed town like this one. You've got to get out, travel a bit while you're young and see the country. If you get into business and make a little cash you can have that. I always knew that I never wanted to work for anyone but me, and now I don't. I have my own business, I still have properties, but not as many, and I can do whatever I want. And I have a feeling, Danny, that you could have that too some day."

"I have to say," I said, "it does sound...perfect."

"Listen, son," Frank said. "Money doesn't buy happiness—it *is* happiness. It's real freedom. Don't let anyone tell you different, no matter how big his head is."

I imagined myself wearing a suit, walking down the streets of Columbus like I owned the place. I would work in a big corner office. I would have a view of the entire city. I would adjourn each evening to The Room and congregate with other men in suits, other big shots who ruled the world.

"You won't have to do it like Vincent and I did it," Big Frank continued. "Go on to law school or business school, Danny. Get educated. Wear that white collar. Some day you'll be writing leases or executing mergers instead of walking through shithole houses on the east side."

Big Frank presided over his empire like a king. His construction company always had business and he rarely knew a year with red ink. The bottom rung of society comprised his workers: drug addicts, felons, high school dropouts, and the occasional illegal immigrant. He paid them almost nothing because he knew he could replace them in an instant. Some of his workers even lived in his Section VIII housing developments.

It was almost as though Big Frank had revived feudalism with Uncle Sam's blessing. On Thanksgiving, he gave turkeys to his favorite tenants in, I suppose, a mark of lordly

138

statesmanship. He played the common man but ruled him. He wore his success with the subtle dignity of his generation. He dressed modestly, drove an expensive car unassumingly, and spoke colloquially. He may have had little more than a high school education, but he was more informed than any economics major I ever met. He followed urban development theory with zeal and had his own take on the rise and fall of cities.

"It moves in cycles," Frank told me once, "first whites own the houses and live happily in them; then, the whites move out and the blacks move in and neighborhoods go to hell. The Jews in the banks seize the houses because the shines can't pay the mortgage. Then other whites like me or Vincent come back in and buy the houses for nothing from the bank, fix them up, and rent them out to either blacks or spics. You can never rent out to whites—they expect too much."

As part of Vinny's education in the world of real estate, Frank took him along to inspect properties he had a mind to buy. Once, about a year before when the recession first rocked America, he took me along as well. It was a modest place on the east side of Columbus, in an acceptable neighborhood that had once been the picturesque home to suburbanites during the 1950s and 60s. Now the once-bright homes and manicured shrubs had waned to a dolorous display of the middle class: faded paint, broken shudders, and lawns strewn with litter.

The house Frank had spotted seemed like all the rest of the block except for the boarded-up windows. The inside revolted me: clothes festered in the middle of the room and piles of feces lay in corners while cockroaches feasted on dead cats. In the bathroom, bleach and ammonia caked the floor where homeless drug addicts had baked crystal meth. Hypodermic needles were strewn across the floor along with matches, pop bottles, and batteries.

"This isn't so bad," Frank muttered in the bathroom. "I've seen them where the bathtub is filled with shit too." It smelled as though a hundred cats had pissed in the place, and Vinny and

I covered our faces to keep from gagging. Big Frank merely lit a cigarette.

"Jesus, Frank," said Vinny, "what the hell are we doing here anyway? How are we going to flip a place like this when the economy is tanking?"

Big Frank continued his inspection of the house. He spoke without care, almost absentmindedly.

"In ancient Rome," he said, "there were two kinds of people: the poor plebeians and the wealthy patricians. The rich and the poor, as they are commonly remembered, but it didn't start out like that. You know when the patricians took over the city?"

"No," I said. Vinny and I paused for the lesson.

"It was during the worst crisis in the Early Republic," Frank said, examining the place's furnace, "while Hannibal was terrorizing all of Italy. When Hannibal got to Rome, all the farmers who lived outside of the walls panicked and fled into the city for protection. Once they were inside, they couldn't leave because they would be killed, but, since they were farmers, they couldn't support themselves or trade inside the city, either."

"So, what happened?" said Vinny.

Big Frank smiled. "The aristocrats knew the farmers needed money for food, and the only thing the farmers had to offer was their land. The patricians were cunning; they knew that Hannibal couldn't stay in Italy forever, and one day the war would be over, so they took a temporary loss and bought the farmer's land—at a reduced price of course."

Vinny and I eyed Frank eagerly, like two schoolboys listening to their favorite instructor.

"Eventually," Frank continued, "Hannibal withdrew and was defeated. The crisis was over, and the patricians controlled all of the land outside of Rome. They let the farmers return to work it, of course, but it wasn't theirs anymore, and the patricians quadrupled their worth. You see, boys, times don't have to be booming to make a profit, even if it is a year or two down the road."

And just like that, the dilapidated house transformed to us. Frank would make money off this place. During a time when the entire country suffered through the worst economic crisis since The Depression, Frank would still turn a profit. He would buy the house from the bank for peanuts, have his workers gut it, refurbish it, and charge twelve hundred a month in rent. Genius. Economists call this sort of thing "Creative Destruction," but I doubt they had ever seen anything like this. I wondered who the first family was to live in that house, what dreams they had, what kind of suppers they made, if they were happy. But I knew it didn't matter.

Listening to Frank at the bar, I thought it all made sense. I wanted to buy my happiness and depend on no one else for it. I wanted to be like Vinny. I knew he would be rich one day and I would be left out. I had to get in The Room where I belonged; I had to be a patrician. I needed to be bold, get mine, and get out of life a man with no debts, regrets, or wishful thinking.

"Well, boys," said Big Frank, yawning, "I think I'm going to be hitting the road. It's time for this old man to get home."

Vinny and I said our goodbyes to Frank, and we ordered another drink. We were drunk, not only because of the booze, but drunk also on Big Frank's stories. Vinny was ecstatic.

"We've got to go right now, Danny—downtown, not the sissy college bars, but some classy joints with classy broads. We're both dressed well enough and I got the cash to pick some up. We've gotta start living man, grab life by the balls and get out there. Next week, we'll drive to Philly, and the week after that, Boston. We have to stop doing the little kid stuff and start being men, like Frank said."

"Fuckin'-A."

We left Flanagan's in Vinny's Cadillac and drove to the classiest joint in town, simply called "The Bar," as if there were no others. As soon as I walked in, I felt cheap. I thought I was losing money just standing in the place. The dimly lit bar had a piano player and no more than twenty clients. Audis, Ferraris, and limousines were lined up outside. *So this is elegance*, I thought. This was what being classy looked like. Some men wore suits, others didn't. One guy sitting at the bar wore a felt jumpsuit; he was an old guy with long white hair. He had a young woman with him, a call girl, loud and drunk. I felt sorry for the two of them.

Vinny ordered a whiskey while I lapped water to sober up, and we sat down near a table of older women who eyed us immediately. I engaged them in conversation. They were in town visiting from Florida.

"Why the hell would you leave Florida to come see Ohio?" Vinny asked. They laughed and said they were in town for a work conference. Dentists. "Seriously," Vinny continued, "if I lived in Florida I would never leave, especially to visit Ohio."

The women lost interest in Vinny quickly. I kept talking to a few of them about Florida and Ohio. I wasn't interested in them, but I wanted to keep conversation going. Vinny was hitting on a woman in a gray pantsuit. She looked haughty and unattractive, but Vinny didn't care.

"You know I got a Cadillac parked outside. I buy houses too. I'm going to own my own neighborhood soon. Not bad for only being twenty-one, huh?"

No one was impressed, and they began talking amongst themselves.

"Piss on it," Vinny told me, "let's ditch these broads and head home."

Vinny got up and tripped over the chair. The women laughed and asked if he needed any help.

"Go to hell," Vinny said. "You broads aren't my mother even though you're all old enough to be." He stormed out and left me to apologize.

"I'm sorry about that," I said. "Normally, he's a real treat." The women thanked me, and apologized that I had to leave. I
142

went outside to find Vinny.

"What the hell was that?" I asked him.

"Screw them, man," he said, stumbling. "Let's get out of here."

"You really need to work on your people skills, buddy."

"I don't need them," he said. "I don't need anybody. I have enough money to not need people skills."

I rolled my eyes as we headed towards his car. Rain trickled down on us and I felt cold. We got to the Cadillac. Vinny grabbed for his keys and dropped them on the ground. Reaching for the keys, he stumbled again and fell. He retrieved them, cursing, and opened the door.

"Get in," he said.

"Let's call a cab," I pleaded.

"No."

"Let me drive."

"Get your own Cadillac, Danny. There's no way I'm letting *you* drive *my* car."

"This is stupid, Vinny."

"Get in the goddamn car or walk home."

He scared me then. I saw that hard, mean look of ignorance in my friend that I remembered in my father, my father who arrived home near dawn, drunk, and skulked away at noon while I was at school, the man who told me, "school is for pussies," the man who told me I would never amount to anything, that I would be a bum like him. But still I wanted to believe in Vinny, to trust him. I wanted to know there was something real about our friendship outside of loneliness and ambition. I got in the car.

We zoomed through downtown, my heart in my throat. The streets were soaked and Vinny was furious that somehow things weren't adding up the way he thought they should have.

"I hate this town," he said. "All my life I've lived in boring Columbus. Everyone here is worthless, so uptight, so formal. I've got to get out of here. We're wasting our lives in this hellhole, Danny. Pretty soon we're going to be old men. We have to make enough money and get out of here, man."

Then two full minutes with nothing but the sound of rain and the hum of that black Cadillac.

"When did it get like this?" said Vinny. "When did we get so old?"

"I've always felt old," I said. "I don't think we chose it. Life just hit us hard, I think."

"I never chose it either. I guess it's my old man's doing too. Nothing I did was ever good enough, you know? I'd make a tackle, and he'd blame it on luck. I'd make some money, but not enough 'to live on.' I remember when he would take me around those houses he used to buy to show me what happens to men without jobs, or respect, or dignity. He told me his was the only way to live. Make money and not have to take shit from anyone." He sighed, and I saw a look of exasperation on his face, as though he had finally stopped pretending. "But sometimes it all seems so, so—"

"Meaningless," I said, more to myself than him.

Vinny's expression changed. His brow furrowed. His eyes narrowed. The car moved faster. I clenched the armrest tighter.

"I remember him putting me into football, into lacrosse, into hunting, fishing, and the Canadian wilderness where we used to go camping—'Men's Camping Trips,' he used to call them."

The rain was picking up now, pouring. The Cadillac's wipers beat in vain against the furious downpour. I was scared. Vinny took no notice and continued.

"'You're going to public school, Vinny, like I did. It'll toughen you up.' Always the same. 'You've got to take over the business one day, Vinny,' he'd say. 'I can't have you be soft.' What if I never wanted that to begin with? What if I wanted to be someone else? He never asked me what I thought about it." The Cadillac moved faster and faster. My heart was pounding, my brow damp with sweat.

"Vinny, we've been drinking. Slow down, goddammit."

"If you can't drive drunk," he said, "don't drive at all. That's what Frank told me. I can do it. Everything is under con—"

The Cadillac hit a slick spot and climbed over a median, tumbling over grass, concrete and debris as the car spun out of control. Vinny hit the brakes hard and we smashed into a dumpster. Vinny screamed.

The Cadillac stopped. Vinny and I were unscathed. We got out and surveyed the damage. The driver's side door was dented, two tires were flat, and the hood of the beautiful car was smashed in like an accordion. Vinny cursed the road, the weather, and the city of Columbus for undoing his beloved Cadillac. I looked at that ruined vehicle and saw all my abject dreams piled within it.

Vinny laughed, crazy laughter, forced and pained. "Don't worry, Danny," he said. "I've got insurance. Everything can be fixed, right? All you need is cash."

I looked at him and shook my head.

"No," I said. "Not everything."

Vinny would pay to have it fixed. He could pay to have anything fixed, anything but himself. Vinny would go on that way forever—rich but bankrupt, and lost. Somehow I knew that. I pitied him. I pitied myself.

I walked away from Vinny that night as the skies of Columbus wept on us, and I was glad for it. We'd wished our youths away so recklessly, so aimlessly, trying so hard to be men.

John P. Deever

John Deever grew up in Westerville, Ohio–a third-generation resident–and graduated from Otterbein College in 1990.

After receiving his M.A. in English from The Ohio State University in 1992, he joined the Peace Corps as a member of the first group of English teachers in newly independent Ukraine.

After living in California, Boston, southern Russia, and Washington, D.C., where his children were born, he returned to central Ohio.

He currently writes for the *Ohio State Alumni Magazine*, *Santa Clara Magazine*, *(614)* magazine, and other venues. His recent essay "Back in the USSR" appeared in Volume Three of *50 Years of Amazing Peace Corps Stories*, titled *A Small Key Opens Big Doors: The Heart of Eurasia.*

WHERE'S JACOB?

By John P. Deever

In his experience, plumbers were rarely talkative, but this one—who was under the bathroom sink fixing the drain he'd broken trying to unclog it—had a lot to say.

"I worked in Tennessee for fourteen years," the plumber said. "Loved my job. Nice weather. Swore I'd never move back here. But, here I am!" His winning laugh left Ben unprepared for what he said next.

"People leave Columbus, but they always end up coming home someday. Right?"

That was true—for Ben anyway, newly returned to Ohio from Washington, D.C., where he ran a micro-finance program for poor farmers in Central Asia. Months spent in villages in Kyrgyzstan and Tajikistan showed him how much he had always taken for granted. How much a person can lose and still find a way to be happy. Because the farmers, high in the Tien Shan, *were*, for the most part, happy, despite long days climbing in high altitude, no running water, and cold winters. He missed the clear, cobalt blue skies over Lake Issyk-Kul. But Ben couldn't explain all that to the plumber.

"Well, it's a nice, safe place to raise kids," he responded, the commonplace thought embarrassingly banal despite being true. "My daughter's five, and my boy is three."

"My three are in high school," the chatty plumber said, tightening a PVC nut on the now—so quickly!—repaired pipe. As a new homeowner in a charming but challenging Victorian off Neil Avenue near The Ohio State University campus, Ben realized he was going to have to get better at home repair. At a lot of things, actually.

"You still gotta watch what they're up to, but it's better than living with toddlers. You can't talk to or reason with the toddlers. They just need a swat on the butt."

"Mm-hmm," he nodded, disagreeing silently as he always tended to do with people who were fixing something in his house. A contractor could say Rush Limbaugh had grown angel wings and flown up to heaven and Ben would probably say, "Oh really?"

He ran the tap and looked underneath for a long time, watching for any sign of an unlikely leak after his competent, thorough work. He stared at the seals not proudly so much as with boredom. He did it every day. Probably, he barely had to pay attention.

"You're all set," the plumber said, wiping his hands and packing up his tools. "You did the right thing. Most people, once they start breaking something, they keep breaking it worse instead of stopping right there, and calling *me*."

Ben nodded gratefully. He envied how this plumber had the world figured out, or believed he did, anyway. He wanted to remember all the man's pronouncements.

"Anyway, welcome back," he added with another laugh.

The playground at Goodale Park was empty, as usual, but Ben's children, Maya and Jacob, didn't mind. The play equipment had a rope bridge, a little slide, and swings off to the side. The bigger kid playground nearby had even more things to climb up, but Maya and Jacob still liked the one for preschoolers. He had no idea then how that play equipment would soon become the location of what Maya would call "the worst day of your life."

After leaving D.C., Ben and his wife, Diane, had marveled at how small, safe, and secure Columbus felt. For Ben, it evoked the safety of his childhood. Diane, who had grown up on the East Coast, marveled like most Easterners that flyover country had some good restaurants. Together they'd hit North Market every Saturday morning and, though they missed some of the sophistication and thrill of Washington, they didn't miss the bars on their first-floor apartment windows, or the police cars and screaming motorcycles escorting motorcades every day, or, after 9/11, the regular thrum of Army helicopters buzzing up and down the Potomac from Langley to the Pentagon.

And then moving home, Ben remembered familiar, reassuring things he had forgotten. Like the train sounding its lovely, low hoot while slowing and creaking through downtown Columbus. A sound that for Ben had once meant freedom and travel now brought only swells of nostalgia to his heart. The dark purple lilacs in his mother's yard still smelled as sweet and delicious as they always had. For a while even the perpetually gray cottage-cheese sky did not depress him or make him wish for the high, bright firmament over Kyrgyzstan.

The Ohio sky. A soft, bumpy blanket, swaddling innocent Buckeyes and reminding them that, while others may soar, they are fated to tread low—their days never marching toward epic triumph but luckily, also rarely to catastrophe. Ben liked to joke, "Thurber said, 'Columbus is a town in which almost everything already has happened.'" Perhaps he should have added, "So nothing much will now."

At least that's how it seemed in Goodale Park with nobody around. Maya and Jacob happily ran and squealed, or when they got tired, paused to make imaginary pancakes and brownies of the mulch under the slide together. Ben looked out at the traffic streaming down I-670 and wondered how he had gotten here.

It was as if the world had moved forward in time, yet nothing was different from 1991, when he had left. A Bush in the White House. A war in Iraq. And, somehow even more inexplicably, Duran Duran still on the radio. Was the universe kidding? All those narrow mountain trails and smiling Asian sheepherders, the corners of their narrow eyes wrinkled and sunburned, all a dream?

"Daddy," Maya said, "can we go over to the big slides?"

"Yeah!" cheered little Jacob—who still wanted, mostly, whatever his sister wanted. Their little angel—the easy baby, textbook in every way, cried when hungry or wet and that was about it. A giggle whose power to make Diane fall over laughing in contagious hilarity seemed like the greatest gift a person could receive. Ah, Jacob. Ben grabbed his bag and followed them as they ran full-speed for the other playground.

Maya and Jacob were the proof that time had moved. When they tired of the big playground, he would push them home quickly in the secondhand double stroller so he could get Jacob out of it before he dropped off for his nap. He was always a good napper too—out like a light, as they say.

So in the story of this fine June day, Ben and Diane and their beloved children walked over to Comfest—Columbus's volunteer-run community music festival of hippies, beer trucks, multiple stages, and big crowds. Since most days the kids had Goodale Park all to themselves, Maya and Jacob were surprised to see so many people in a place they halfway believed belonged solely to them. In fact, Ben felt the same way.

But the Comfest vibe was always great—the crowds somehow both happy and serene. People were lying around on blankets listening to bands, joking, laughing loud. Or dancing— like those two barefoot hippie girls in tank tops and flowing skirts. *It's Comfest,* Ben thought. *What a really good vibe.*

When they got to the play equipment, it was swarming with kids—sixty maybe? Every nook and cranny, little arms and legs in motion. Maya and Jacob jumped right in—the more the merrier, on a playground too often desolate and empty. Diane and Ben stood nearby, enjoying the music on the Main Stage in the distance, and watching.

And then, up walked the kids' pediatrician, Doctor Terri— the only doctor anyone in the family ever looked forward to visiting. Ben spoke admiringly of Dr. Terri's tie-dyed shirt. He'd only ever seen her in a doctor's coat.

The four adults talked about Comfest a little, and how funny it was to meet there outside the office, as friends. Later, Ben couldn't remember that part too well, because the next thing Terri said was, "Where's Jacob?"

Ben saw Maya at the top of the slide, but he couldn't see Jacob anywhere in the scrum of kids. But surely he was just underneath, in the mulch again? Diane walked closer, peering under, while Ben walked around to look up into the tube slide where neither of them could see. Terri looked around back on the climbing wall. No one saw him.

And then Diane took Maya's hand.

Ben's heart beat faster than it ever had, and his face tingled, and the panic began, and his mind said, *don't worry, he's right here, you just saw him,* and his heart pounded out *yes, yes he is, it must, it must be so.*

Ben's hands shook, and he began to scramble. The Comfest crowd was huge. The park was full of people. They could be anywhere by now.

They.

No—come on. It's Comfest, there's a really good vibe, he struggled to remember, *and of all places it's the last place somebody would go if they...*

They.

Ben pictured three-year-old Jacob, in the purple T-shirt he wore that day. The perfect, golden boy. And suddenly he knew it. He just knew. In fact, now it was all clear: he had always known. The boy was too good to be true, and now he was gone. *Here it is,* his heart said, *and you always knew it. You knew one day the unspeakable would befall him.*

Diane's face showed the same thing, but she wisely said, "I'll take Maya over to the big kids' playground. Maybe he went there."

"He knows he's not allowed to go over without asking," Ben said.

Diane held Maya's hand tightly.

"Mommy," their daughter asked. "Is this the worst day of your life?"

Diane paused. "I don't know yet, honey."

Of course. Here was fate—to come home not to hometown safety but the worst robbery imaginable. A nice, safe place for kids! *Why, oh why, had we thought to come here,* his mind screamed, *or at least why had we ever let a single moment go by when he was out of our sight?* It took only a few seconds. Ben's eyes jumped from child to child, searching for Jacob, his Jacob, here a moment ago—then gone? How easy it was for them, they, them, to scoop up a trusting three-year-old and inconspicuously walk away, walk steadily straight out of the park. And on to—

Ben's mind could not do that, not yet, could not go that far. As he watched Diane and Maya head for the other playground, he ran in circles around the area, checking every group, staring in despair at every face. Was it *you*? Or *you*? He ran and looked up and down, then scanned the horizon for an adult carrying a child. He ran across the parking lot he had always made sure the kids avoided, though every day except this one it had always been empty and unused. The band on the stage brought a final song to a crashing end. Ben could not reason through the overtaking panic.

Maya and Diane had reached the other playground now. He could see them way over there, searching, and they looked small and distant in the dense crowd.

"Jacob!" he yelled, "Jacob!"

Maybe the boy would hear his father's call now that the band had stopped. The circles of Ben's anxious roving widened, quickened; people began staring; but he could not speak except to shout "Jacob!" Unable to think, even hear. "My three-year-old," Ben cried silently, "my toddler!"

He half-heard words, coming from the stage: "...in a purple shirt..."

Ben ran to the stage and grabbed the first volunteer he found, still not seeing his son anywhere.

And then a paramedic was there, and he was speaking, and nodding.

"Yes, we found him. Go over to the Lost Kids area."

The firefighter holding Jacob in the Lost Kids area was asking him questions which Jacob did not answer. From the firefighter's arms, Ben took his three-year-old son in that now unforgettable tiny purple shirt, and suddenly he was crying, squeezing, repeating Jacob's name. Jacob had been silent up until then, but now he was crying too.

"Jacob!" the firefighter said. "So that's your name. You wouldn't talk till Daddy showed up, eh? Jacob's my name too, how about that?"

Ben still could barely breathe or speak.

"I saw you coming a mile away," the firefighter laughed. "I could tell you were the dad by the way you leaped over that fence."

Clutching Jacob, Ben ran to find Diane and Maya as fast as he could; Diane's agony had lasted a few moments longer. Maya scolded her little brother for upsetting everybody—as if *Jacob* had done anything wrong.

Ben was sure he hadn't wandered off far. *I know my kid*, he thought. *Some well-meaning Comfest patron took him there. Perhaps he strayed a little from the play equipment, looking for us. Our conversation with Dr. Terri had been only seconds. Maybe somebody thought they were doing a good deed. They.*

In the end, for Ben and Diane, not the worst day of their lives. But some of the worst minutes.

People leave Columbus, but they always end up home, the plumber had said. "That 'always' isn't quite right," Ben said later.

Perhaps it *is* true that in Columbus everything has happened, so nothing much will now. Perhaps that's not so bad after all.

Brad Pauquette

Brad Pauquette loves Columbus, however, it's yet to be seen if the feeling is mutual.

He lives in Woodland Park, an inner-city neighborhood on Columbus' Near-East Side, with his wife, Melissa, his son, Theodore, and a dog named Harvey. Together, they're slowly rehabbing their house, and doing their best to appreciate all of the miraculous gifts God provides for them each day.

To pay the bills, Brad works as an independent web developer and consultant, specializing in helping small businesses and micro-enterprises establish a sustainable, cost-effective presence on the internet. You can find more information about his work at www.BradPauquetteDesign.com.

The first draft of "Self Fulfillment" was a simple morality tale based on a biblical parable. Thanks to the tremendous insight and efforts of his fellow CCC workshoppers, the story has been washed and complexified into something entirely better.

Brad would like to thank his family for putting up with yet another project, and the fantastic group that is Columbus Creative Cooperative, whose collective efforts have produced three magnificent anthologies in 2011.

154

SELF FULFILLMENT
By Brad Pauquette

It was Dr. Adam Grossman's big day.

"It's my big day," he told his wife, Barbara, as they stood backstage and listened to the hubbub of reporters filing in and taking their seats in the auditorium. "All the years of study pay off in this."

"It's time, dear," she said, pecking him dutifully on the cheek and sliding her slender body through the small gap she'd parted in the curtains.

Adam was left alone backstage, with his hands folded in front of him at his waist, his fingers ticking nervously on the knuckles of the opposite hand. He could picture his wife on the other side of the curtain, standing confidently behind the wooden podium, with the tremendous machine covered in a sheet only a few feet to her left.

"Thank you all for coming today," he heard his wife's voice reverberating off of the rear walls of the auditorium and muffled through the heavy curtain. "This is a very important day for my husband and me. Dr. Grossman has worked tirelessly for decades now to devise the technology that stands beside me.

"With no further ado, I present the distinguished Dr. Adam Grossman, M.D., Ph.D, PsyD, neuroscientist and expert robotics engineer." Her voice rose in pitch and volume with emphasis as she traversed the impressive list of credentials.

The audience applauded amiably while Adam parted the curtains and graced the stage.

Richard Winger, AP reporter in the fourth row, applauded alongside them, but for Barbara's impressive performance, not out of respect for Dr. Adam Grossman.

"Thank you, again, for coming today," Dr. Grossman began, his voice trembling only slightly. So slightly that perhaps only he and Richard Winger noticed it.

"I'd especially like to thank The Ohio State University and

155

its generous administration that has made this project a reality, as well as my advisers, Dr. Werner, Dr. Regal and Dr. Hopewell. The university's phenomenal medical research department, combined with the burgeoning tech development and robotics industry in the area made the beautiful city of Columbus, Ohio the ideal place to pursue this project. Also, thank you to my lovely wife, Barbara, who introduced me today, and who has stood by me through the shortest days and longest years of our lives while I developed this.

"Imagine, if you will," he continued, "as we embark on the colonization of Mars, as the fluctuations in our climate threaten our food supply, as genetic science advances, if we had a way to calculate the finest men among us. Who should propagate the species? Who is qualified by character, integrity and ambition to take the highest posts and lead the finest offices on our globe? Who should live and who should die, who should be spared from calamity?"

The auditorium sat silently as Dr. Grossman walked over to the sheet-covered object that shared his stage.

"These are questions of the past!" he shouted as he pulled the cover from the machine. The crowd applauded diligently as the sheet fell, revealing a cylindrical apparatus ten feet tall and six feet in diameter. The nondescript stainless steel contraption was open in the front, with a cavity inside large enough to hold a man standing upright. The exterior and interior walls of the machine were constructed of rivetless, smooth metal panels that reflected the stage lights. The monstrous cylinder's only ornament was a glass display panel on the outside, just to the side of the opening.

"May I introduce to you," he shouted over the applause, "EVA, the world's first Electronic Value Assessment machine."

His speech hit its stride, and he confidently basked in the applause of the reporters who sat before him, the natural critics who could make or break the public opinion of his life's innovation.

As the applause died down, he began again. "The year 2019 will be remembered as the year that humanity left careless judgment behind. Discrimination is a thing of the past. Prejudice no longer serves a purpose.

"EVA is better than you and I. She has no bias, she does not pander and she has no vanity. When a man walks into this machine to be scanned, two minutes later EVA simply supplies a numerical value of that man's worth."

Dr. Adam Grossman was delighted to hear skeptical grumbles from the audience.

"How can this be, you ask?" he goaded them. "Through advances in neuroscience, EVA can scan your brain to determine your intelligence, your propensity for violence, even your most critical motives and ethical nature. A scan of your body reveals your fitness level and longevity, and detects your likelihood of developing fatal or expensive medical problems."

It was darkness from Adam's perspective beyond the first few rows, but even then he could see a few heads nod, and a few suspicious glares turn to confused stares.

"Thanks to the digitization of all government records, this information is cross-referenced with all of the data available on the individual. Criminal record, standardized test scores, medical records, accomplishments and meritorious awards, military service, and on and on.

"In only two minutes, EVA can understand the individual better than he understands himself!"

Silence hung over the room while the reporters absorbed the information.

"No need to save them until the end, perhaps I can answer a few questions now," the doctor offered to the crowd, to their relief. He motioned with his hand for the house lights to be brought up. As soon as the lights were on, he saw a dozen hands in the air, though they remained respectfully silent.

"Yes, you there." He indicated the reporter he'd talked to the evening before.

"Clarkson, *Columbus Dispatch.* How can you possibly establish a reliable rubric for a human being?"

"Excellent question, thank you," Grossman began. "The machine is adaptive. The average score will always be fifty, and a bell curve is applied to the entire spectrum, zero to one hundred. We've calibrated it with a random cross section of society thus far—everyone from criminals to priests. Good people, too," he joked, "like school teachers and newspaper reporters."

He paused while the audience chuckled.

"The numbers will change and recalibrate progressively, and should more than one machine ever exist, it's already set up to network for global calibration."

"Dr. Grossman!" someone shouted from across the room.

Grossman instinctively looked towards the voice and said, "Yes?" but immediately kicked himself. He couldn't lose control of the room so quickly. He momentarily grimaced and squeezed his fingers into a fist, but recaptured his composure without hesitation.

"What's the cost of this machine?" the young woman asked without identifying herself.

"Future machines can be manufactured at an estimated 1.4 million dollars," he answered politely.

"Yeah, but what about this one?" she fired back.

"This project was finished under budget at fourteen million dollars."

Richard Winger was already speaking before Grossman finished the word "dollars."

"And if we count the last twenty years you've been 'studying' and 'tinkering' on the taxpayers' dime? How much then? Forty million? Sixty?"

"Mr. Winger." Grossman hesitated only a moment. "I'm surprised to hear from you so soon. Do you intend to impugn all of those in the room who have studied without cost, or only me?"

"How many scholarship holders do we have in the room today?" Grossman continued, uninterrupted. Nervous chuckles filled the room as one of every four hands climbed into the air. "Come on now," he chided, "PELL grants? GI Bill? Gift from the rotary club, anyone? Reduced lunch program?" He chuckled as the few remaining hands rose into the air. "We can't all jet-set around the world looking at and writing about things. Some of us take action to make the world a better place.

"How about a demonstration?" he asked. The audience dropped their hands into their laps and nodded their approval. "How about my lovely wife?"

Barbara had disappeared stage left when Grossman began his speech, but she reappeared now, coolly and confidently approaching the machine.

"The lady will step inside the machine," he explained as she did so. "I'll simply hit this button on the command module, and the robotics will do the rest."

He hit the button, and much to the reporters' disappointment, there was no whizzing or humming, giga-watts of electricity did not zap from one side of the cylinder to the other. If they had listened closely, they might have heard a delicate hum, and the occasional click like that of a camera shutter.

"Right now the machine is verifying her identity based on photos from the BMV, her staff ID from anywhere she's ever been employed and her high school yearbook. Fresh dental x-rays are not only confirming her name and social security number, but assisting the machine in determining her overall health, nutrition, her body's longevity, and even her nervous habits.

"A bone density scan, a mammogram and a full-body CT scan are all happening simultaneously, and will be instantly analyzed for anomalies. A brain scan will commence right now—" he snapped his fingers. Barbara's eyes shut, then her face contorted in pain, then anguish, followed by tribulation, then nausea. She laughed uncontrollably for a mere moment

159

and then wept like a baby.

"She won't remember any portion of this section. She is effectively comatose while under the control of the machine," Grossman explained while his wife's face competed in the expression Olympics, enduring gnashing of teeth and bitter rage. "The machine is simulating the introduction of a vast array of stimuli to further test her neuro-electrical responses. With each simulated toxin, each contrived situation that we introduce, EVA can detect exactly how her brain responds. Does her brain respond with the areas isolated for rage, prejudice, mockery? Does her brain trigger her to flee or to fight? EVA is testing each and every possibility, as well as testing the results against the accumulated adversity of her life."

Just as suddenly as it started, Barbara's face became expressionless and her eyes opened. The machine dinged gently and she smiled at the audience.

"The scan is complete," he told them. "Please step out, Barbara."

She complied, and waved amicably as she did.

"How do you feel, Barbara?"

"So fantastically relaxed," she exclaimed at once, gushing. "Truly fantastic. Unbelievably complete and emotionally validated, more satisfied than I've been in years—"

He cut her off. "Thank you, Barbara. Ready for your score?"

She nodded her head and gracefully released a long accumulated sigh.

"Sixty-five!" he shouted. Though he'd learned her score when they tested the machine months earlier, his inward disappointment still belied his triumphant tone. "You are a human being far above average!"

The crowd of journalists and reporters applauded, and for the first time, Grossman noticed that some of them were taking notes.

"How about *your* score?" Richard Winger's voice echoed

around the auditorium.

"I'm not taking questions right now," Grossman said, waving him off. "Now that we know her score, in the future our legislative officials can use this information to make a more just society. The machine can even be used to determine spousal compatibility."

"How do we know it's accurate?" Winger's voice broke forth again. "The machine could have said anything."

"I said no questions! Please!" Grossman spurted, popping his 'p' into the microphone, his knuckles whitening as he gripped the podium. He exhaled and resumed, "With the help of modern statistics, EVA can practically predict the future."

"But sixty-five is the perfect number!" Winger objected, rising from his seat. "High enough to not be embarrassing, low enough to not arouse suspicion. It could give everyone a sixty-five for all we know!"

Winger's colleagues laughed, followed by a collective grumbling that spread across the room like an ego-eating bacteria.

"Well! What now! That's ridiculous. I say! What!" The distinguished doctor morphed into a stammering idiot in front of them. He went silent and collected himself. "I am a decorated scientist, Mr. Winger, I assure you."

"Wrong! You're a career student! For what other advancements of the sciences have you been decorated good 'doctor'?" Winger taunted him, playfully. "You've, possibly impressively, Frankensteined a collection of technological advances together. But all I've seen is your wife standing inside a fourteen million dollar cylinder that appears to do nothing, and then you announce 'sixty-five'."

Grossman's shoulders slumped. In more than seven hundred academic hours of advanced studies, he'd never taken public speaking.

Winger had the kill, but he wasn't ready yet.

"I'm not suggesting you're a fraud, Dr. Grossman," he

conceded after the room recomposed itself. "But as a member of the journalistic community, I'm simply asking you to prove it."

Grossman scoffed.

"Your score, doctor?" Winger queried.

"Who would run the machine?" Grossman's face brightened. "I've a better idea. How about we find yours, Mr. Winger?"

In his right mind, Winger would have objected, but instead he seized the opportunity to join Barbara and the doctor on stage. Leaving his jacket in his seat, he hustled to the front of the auditorium and bounced up the four steps to take his place in the spotlight.

He hadn't been this close to Barbara since the day sixteen years earlier when he had kissed her in the terminal of the Columbus airport.

"It's just a year," Barbara had told him before he boarded his flight, as she stood pressed against him amidst the bustling crowd. "Don't get your life too started without me."

"I won't," Ricard Winger had promised. "I'm going to be so busy with the journal I'll barely have time to get things set up for us. They're going to work me like a dog, you know."

"I know," Barbara giggled. "I love you."

Her chin dug into the center of his chest as they embraced. They kissed, and embraced, and kissed.

Richard Winger, fresh out of OSU's journalism department, flew away to New York. He leased a one-bedroom apartment in Manhattan that he couldn't afford, big enough for a couple, just so they were in love. He considered getting a dog, but got a fish instead. He didn't make friends, he thought it would be easier when they were together.

"I've met someone," came Barbara's call three months later. Winger and Barbara had talked every day, but this came without warning. "I think I love him, and I think he's going places."

162

"What?!" Richard yelled into the receiver, something he'd never done before. "I already *am* places!"

That was the last time they'd spoken, the last time they'd seen each other, until this day when Winger grinned and stood next to Barbara Grossman on an auditorium stage at The Ohio State University back in Columbus, Ohio.

"Thank you, Mr. Winger." Grossman extended a hand towards the machine. "If you'll be so kind."

"Side effects?" Winger asked.

Grossman shook his head. Winger walked towards the machine.

"There's only one button!" Winger objected as he walked past the control panel, stopping in his tracks.

"Afraid?" the doctor asked. It was enough to get Winger into the machine. "You should take off your belt."

Winger obliged and handed it to Barbara. She stretched her hand into the cylinder for it, looked into his eyes sympathetically and then towards the ground as she walked away.

"Here we go," Grossman said as he hit the button and the scan began. "You see folks, that's all it takes. There's no prep, no trouble. This single machine could scan more than seven hundred people per day, more than a quarter million people each year."

Winger rolled his eyes.

"As you'll recall, now comes the brain scan," the doctor reminded his audience. Winger's eyes went shut, his face contorted. "There is one minor side effect that we see on occasion...of particular note in male subjects..."

He paused for effect.

"Spontaneous orgasm." Grossman laughed guardedly as the room erupted when the prediction came to fruition. "Of course, we can only speculate as to how his brain was stimulated to cause such a bizarre...reaction," he shouted into the microphone over the raucous crowd. "Perhaps someone could fetch the reporter's coat from his chair."

A young man grabbed the coat and brought it to Barbara onstage, where she reached out for it without prying her eyes from the ground.

A delightful ding sounded, and Winger awakened to a different crowd than he had fallen asleep to, he felt like a contender in a blood sport amidst the commotion.

Dr. Grossman quieted the crowd down with his hands and fetched the coat from Barbara. "Perhaps for around your waist?" the doctor suggested, handing the coat to Winger as he stepped out of the cylinder. Winger's eyes burned with fury when he looked down at his nicely-pressed khakis.

Instead of the applause and laughter Grossman was expecting, the room was silent. Apprehension hung in the air while the news men waited for the conflict to culminate—waited for the story.

But Winger knew better than that, he knew that now he held the room.

"My score, doctor?" he asked calmly, nonchalantly holding his jacket in front of him.

"Of course, reporter," he answered, grinning like a kid on Christmas. He glanced at the screen on the control panel.

"Sixty-five!" he croaked.

This was too good even for Richard Winger, who belted laughter from somewhere deep inside, exhaling so hard he had to grab the side of the machine to keep from falling over. The journalists in the audience followed their new ledaer and laughed into the air, which seemed to be thickening around Grossman. The doctor stared at a spot on the back wall of the auditorium and mumbled inaudibly.

"Coincidence!" Grossman shouted. "It's just a coincidence."

"Of course it is," Winger said, comforting him between wheezing breaths. "Your wife and I are both sixty-fives."

Barbara blushed and turned away from the audience, and Grossman stepped back to the microphone.

"This is how a bell curve works," he explained to the jeering faces. "There are naturally more people who score sixty-five, than, say, one hundred or zero."

A few of them still laughed audibly, but the room began to compose itself.

"Dr. Grossman," Winger interrupted politely. "Perhaps you could explain what it would take for a person to achieve a perfect one hundred."

Taken aback by Winger's apparent assistance, Grossman picked up, "Yes, thank you Mr. Winger. A very good idea indeed. A person who scores a perfect hundred is exceptionally likely to have a positive impact on society as a whole through the course of his life. His chemistry, neuro-makeup, intelligence, moral fortitude and physical capacities make it nearly impossible for him to *not* make the world a better place. Whereas someone who scores a fifty is unlikely to have an effect whatsoever. He simply lives and dies, or through his life oscillates between constructive and destructive behavior towards others."

"I see, very good." Winger nodded his head. "And to score a zero then, someone would have to be exceptionally likely to have a serious negative effect on society as a whole."

"Yes, exactly," Grossman confirmed, surprised by his new ally. "A person who scores a zero is most likely incapable of deciphering between actions that are meant to help others and those that harm them. Either that or he's evil, or completely selfish and egocentric. In reality, it's almost impossible to score either a zero or a one hundred."

"I see." Winger continued to encourage the doctor. "And where would you place yourself, if you had to wager?"

"Oh, I couldn't possibly—"

"Come now, doctor, what score? A sixty-five?"

"Ha!" Grossman laughed. "Well, I can assure you that in previous tests my score was well above fifty."

"Oh, come now," Winger chided him playfully. "Surely

much higher. You've spent your life inventing a machine that will help mankind to separate the good from the bad preemptively, the wheat from the chaff before it has a chance."

"Well, I guess I don't know. It wouldn't be fair to test myself."

"Come now, an eighty? A ninety?"

"Perhaps," Grossman obliged, blushing. "It is truly a fabulous machine."

"Save the world, right doc?" Winger supported him. "Why, I'd say if there's a perfect one hundred in this room, it's probably right here on stage," and he began to applaud.

The reporters in the crowd, though suspicious, still supported their hero and took up applause with him.

"Oh, please." The doctor's face turned red. "It's exceptionally unlikely that there's a one hundred in the room… please, stop. A ninety—I was close to a ninety."

Winger stopped applauding. He looked over at Barbara and winked. Barbara stood with her gaze still fixed on the ground, her hand covered her eyes and a portion of her furrowed brow.

"That's a good score, a very good score. Why not just step inside and prove to this audience that your machine can give a different score, a higher score?" He gestured towards the machine. "Come now, doctor. I'm certain that we can handle hitting a button. We're both sixty-fives, you know."

The doctor held up his hands in protest, but Winger continued, "Come now, doctor, you can even borrow my jacket." The crowd applauded and whistled.

Barbara came close to her husband, leaned in and whispered, "You don't have to, dear, you've absolutely nothing to prove. Don't do it."

"That's enough, Barbara," he admonished her like she was an anxious child. "You ran it before and I scored an eighty-eight, no reason to worry now."

"Your score, doctor?" Winger chimed in.

With that, the doctor acquiesced, took his belt out of his

pants, and handed it to Barbara.

The crowd shouted their approval.

"Just hit the button once," he instructed nervously as he entered the cylinder, turning and smiling at the audience with darting eyes.

"Yes, yes, only once," Winger verified.

"Dear...Adam!" Barbara tried to capture his attention, but he ignored her.

"See you in two minutes, good doctor," Winger told him, and pushed the button on the mammoth apparatus.

Winger and Barbara stood outside the cylinder and watched as Grossman's eyes shut, and his expression began to contort.

"It's nice to see you, Barbara," Richard whispered to her as they waited.

"You're an ass," she whispered back.

"Have you gone the places you expected?"

"What?" she asked.

"You told me he was going places." He hesitated. "When we talked on the phone sixteen years ago, when I was waiting in New York City while you finished school—this school—in Columbus."

"Oh, God," she exhaled. "I don't know. What do you mean by a question like that?"

"What do I mean?" he whispered back. "I guess I mean that we could have gone places. I mean that..." He paused, and abandoned himself. "I just mean that it's nice to see you."

EVA dinged and the doctor came to, his eyes flashed to the front of his pants, which were still clean. He chuckled and stepped out of the chamber.

"Very good then," he chuckled as he put his hand on the cylinder and looked admiringly at the stainless steel machine. "You're quite something, EVA, quite something."

Grossman looked up from his invention and thought he saw a pained look in his wife's eyes. But as soon as he noticed it, it was already gone.

"And for my score, Mr. Winger?"

Barbara and Winger looked at the display panel. Barbara's eyes fell and she placed her hand over her mouth. Winger looked purely surprised—simply shocked.

"You're certain this machine is accurate?" Winger asked.

"Indeed," the doctor responded indignantly.

"You'd stake your career on it," Winger asked. "You'd bet your life?"

Barbara jumped in. "There are still bugs to work out. It's not one hundred percent yet."

"Barbara! EVA's perfect—the most perfect thing in the world," he reiterated. "She's beautiful and rational."

"You're certain?"

"My score, Mr. Winger?"

Barbara and Winger stared at the instrument panel in silence, then looked back to the doctor, then to the instrument panel.

"My score!"

Winger pursed his lips and continued to look at him.

"BARBARA! WHAT IN GOD'S NAME IS MY SCORE?"

But she simply shook her head, then covered her face again and began to cry.

Grossman pushed them out of the way with his shoulder and stopped with his nose six inches from the display panel.

"Oh God," he muttered, and fell to his knees. "Oh God, no, EVA...no...this can't be right. EVA, why?"

Richard Winger, AP, suddenly remembered that they were onstage in front of a room full of hundreds of reporters.

"What is it?" one of them shouted.

"A hundred?" somebody asked, and they all laughed.

"Zero?" someone else called out.

Winger looked to the ground. He didn't answer, he simply held up his index finger.

"One?" the same person shouted, and Winger nodded his

head.

Someone in the audience guffawed, another gasped audibly. The inexperienced journalists snickered, but most sat silently, waiting like wolves, unsure how to provoke the best story.

Meanwhile, Grossman leaned against EVA's instrument panel, wallowing in embarrassment. "Why, EVA? After everything? Why?"

"God, Richard, what did you do?" Barbara whispered with fear in her eyes. Winger simply threw his hands up and shook his head.

"Adam, dear," she said, bending down to him. "Please, it's just an error."

"But why now?" he moaned. "Last time you ran it I got an eighty-eight...right?"

Barbara stood beside him, silent.

"Barbara?" He turned his attention fully to her. "I never checked the record, the display panel was still in the other room before we assembled the cylinder. You told me I scored an eighty-eight."

Barbara started to say something, but instead dropped her head into her hands. A stifled sob slipped out between her fingers.

"Did I score an eighty-eight last time?" he insisted.

She simply shook her head, which was still buried in her hands.

"I scored a one and you didn't tell me?" he accused, his temper igniting. "You inconsiderate dullard! Why?"

"Adam, calm down," she said, backing away. "I believed in you, I believe in the project—"

"I'm a ONE, goddammit! You're a sixty-five and I'm a goddamn ONE? It doesn't make sense. I'm Dr. Adam Grossman! You're just my wife! EVA's perfect," he shouted into the ground. "EVA didn't make an error, I did. You're my error!"

"Adam, please." she pleaded, dejected, stepping

backwards. As she backed further away, Winger took her arm.

Grossman sank to the floor, and placed his hand on EVA. He seethed, and beat the wooden stage with his fist. "I'm a zero, I'm a zero, I'm nothing, worthless," he muttered.

"What's he gonna do?" Winger whispered to Barbara while the doctor continued to lament on the floor, but she only shook her head.

"Should we call security or something? He's gonna go berserk."

"He'll be fine," she whispered back.

"Oh God, EVA." Grossman stood. "That's it. I made you. You're my life's work." He touched the machine gently. "The only way I could be detrimental to society, is if...*you're*... detrimental to society."

The doctor paced the stage now, muttering and calculating with his eyes.

"Adam," Barbara pleaded, "maybe we should reschedule." She projected to the audience now. "Ladies and gentlemen, we're going to take a short intermission, please join us again..."

"Shut up, woman!" Grossman yelled. "This is the way it has to be. EVA knows it. Why must you be so dense!?"

Grossman stalked to the microphone, and screamed into it. "STAY! SIT DOWN!" No one moved. "I'M MAKING THE WORLD A BETTER PLACE!"

Without another word, he stormed off stage left. Anxious silence hung heavy in the air. A whisper filled the room as the reporters exchanged the mutual questions that hung among them.

Barbara turned to Winger, and in a hushed voice accused him, "You think I don't know what you're doing, Richard Winger?"

"What are you talking about? I had no idea..."

"No! You've got no business being here."

"I'm a reporter, Barbara. I asked a question," he pleaded.

"Nonsense, Richard," she retorted. "I've read your

articles." Her face turned red. "Genocide in Somalia, riots in Europe, sex slaves in Asia? You've got no business...you came here to make trouble for me."

"You're right, Barbara," he said. "I waited sixteen years to ask your husband a question that I knew would ruin his career."

They were silent on stage again, waiting. All they could do was wait—all anyone could do was wait.

"So what if I wanted to see you?" Winger finally asked.

"What?"

"I see you in the paper, too."

"So?"

"So? I've seen pictures of you...at charity auctions alone, at benefits alone...never mind. You're right, I shouldn't have come here. I've got no goddamn business."

They waited in silence again.

"Where did he go?" she finally asked.

"You tell me, he's your husband."

"I have no idea," she admitted. "Just like always. He's not here, that's all I know." She put her head in her hands, and then she heard him coming.

Dr. Adam Grossman came back on stage carrying a hammer and a pry-bar in one hand, and a wooden baseball bat in the other.

"Adam!" Barbara yelled. "What in God's name are you doing?"

"I think I've heard enough from you today, Barbara!" He threw his words at her, then he turned to his machine as if he and EVA were the only two objects in the world. He set the pry-bar and the baseball bat on the ground, then he patted the metallic cylinder and pressed his cheek against the digital display.

If the reporters listened closely enough they could hear him saying, "Shhh...EVA, you were wonderful..." If they looked closely, they would have seen tears rolling down the scientist's face as he whispered over and over, "I'm sorry, EVA...I'm sorry, EVA. It's not you, it's me."

Barbara stared on—stupefied, horrified, frozen by what she saw before her. She closed her eyes and every muscle in her body tightened in embarrassment and anxiety. She pushed her fingernails into her palm so hard it would have bled if Winger hadn't grabbed her hand to stop her. She opened her eyes and looked up at him.

"I'm sorry, Richard," she whispered through the tears that were forming in her eyes. "Please help me." He saw the eyes of the twenty-two-year-old girl—wild, pleading, alive—that he left in the airport so many years ago, and he needed no more reason.

Winger released her hand, and moved towards Grossman. "Dr. Grossman," he said, placing his hand on his shoulder. "I think that's enough. Let's head backstage, maybe go out for a drink." Winger placed his other hand on the hammer.

"No, get back!" Grossman jerked the hammer away, and pushed Winger backwards into Barbara. "Back with the trickster!"

Then the good doctor breathed deeply and raised the hammer above his head with both hands. He closed his eyes and shrieked as the hammer descended and smashed through the digital display on the side of the cylinder.

He giggled maniacally as he dislodged the hammer from the machine and brought it down again and again into the display. He yelled obscenities as he stepped inside of the cylinder and thrashed about, kicking the metal surface with his feet, hammering at the welded seams in the thin sheeting until they split and wiring spilled from EVA like intestines from a gutted fish.

Barbara grabbed Winger's arm as she watched, clinging to his bicep like a crawdad clings to a stick.

"Oh, God, Richard," she said, her strong will dissolving. "What do we do?"

For too long, Winger had thought of the "we" of she and him. Alone at his kitchen table, four beers into a break up, Barbara was his "what if?" girl, his hostess in that smooth area

172

of content melancholy that comes from unanswerable "if-onlys."

But he'd always returned from that soothing cool zone of self-deprecating fantasy in a stupor the next morning. She, he had imagined, was content without him as he set about the globe from one famished war zone to another. The hard line of a smile graced his face now as this woman clung to his arm, and he remembered his editor's face when he asked to go to Columbus, Ohio to cover a scientific exposé.

Fat Ed Kryzowski, managing editor, who insisted on continuing to smoke in his office and waiting for the fine to roll in, asked him, "You want to go to butt-fuck Ohio for what?"

"It's a metropolis of over three million, Ed, it could be a big deal," Winger had insisted. "Guy says he's invented a machine that can assign accurate digital values to human beings for their societal worth."

Ed stared at him incredulously. "You need a vacation?" he asked him. "Do some red carpet bullshit on the coast. *That* I can sign off on." He smashed the butt of his cigarette into the ash tray, and fumbled to encourage another out of the soft pack. "But this—we'll pick up the story from the goddamn college newspaper if anything comes out of it, blow some nineteen-year-old's load when his story gets picked up by the AP and hashed to shit." Ed lit his cigarette. "Come on, Winger, think about the kids..."

"What do they pay you by the cigarette around here?" Winger asked when Ed shoved his pack towards him. "No thanks. Look Ed, if I go there's a story. Wherever I go, you get a pretty nice story, right?"

"Because we don't send you to goddamn Columbus, Ohio," Ed fired back, dragging in on his cigarette and exhaling a thick cloud of smoke towards the ceiling. He looked Winger up and down, saw that he had no intention of leaving defeated, and his tone softened. "Alright, Winger. What's it gonna take, two days? Just promise me you'll get laid or something."

Now here he was, arm in arm with his college girlfriend,

a woman. But this wasn't the story Ed was going to be thrilled with. The crazed man pulverizing a magical ten-foot cylinder—*that* was the story.

Grossman continued to kick the walls sporadically as the machine fell apart, still spilling electrical components. Millions of dollars of specially adapted, one-of-a-kind medical examination equipment crashed to the floor, glass and plastic amalgamations crunched and crumbled as they spread across the ground.

The audience of news men sat in silence, simply taking it all in. There were no notes to take, no quotes to jot down to break up the factual monotony—this story was writing itself in front of them. The crazed scientist, the distraught wife, the first-class newspaper man with the soiled pants—characters fit for a fable, but made for the newspaper.

"It's plugged in," Winger mumbled as Grossman kicked a wall of the cylinder completely to the floor.

"What?" Barbara asked, engrossed by the swift undoing of her husband before her. "What?"

"It's plugged in!" Winger shouted now, but it was too late. In a cathartic act of destruction, Grossman picked up the pry-bar, hooked a thick bundle of wires with it and pulled with both hands like he was starting an oversized lawnmower.

There was a spark somewhere between his fingertips and the pry-bar, his eyes widened, and he froze as the machine fed power through both of his arms, down his ribcage, torso and legs and into the floor. His body shivered from the impulses, but no circuit breaker tripped, no fuse popped.

Winger snatched the baseball bat from the ground, took two steps and swung the club into the doctor's left shoulder, knocking him free of the machine and sending him sprawling onto the stage.

"Somebody call 9-1-1!" Winger shouted. The young man who had brought up his jacket was already making the call.

Winger and Barbara rushed to Grossman's side. His eyes

were still wide and stimulated.

Winger felt for a pulse and found one.

"Don't move, dear," Barbara instructed him. "Help is coming."

"I'm sorry," Grossman whispered to his wife.

"It's okay," she whispered back, and smiled down at him. "I'm sorry...I should've told you."

"No," he panted. "I'm sorry to EVA. She's brilliant...she knew she had to be destroyed. But tell her I'm sorry...anyway."

Barbara got up and took a step back, her countenance destroyed, face furious. Her fists balled up into iron mallets, she breathed in pulses, and tears blocked her vision. Winger looked back at her, put his hand up as if to say "it's okay," and then turned back to Grossman.

Richard Winger leaned in close and whispered in the doctor's ear, "Wouldn't EVA have known that you were going to destroy her?"

Grossman's eyes went wide in horror, a vein in his forehead pulsed visibly underneath his skin, and he passed out.

Winger checked the doctor's pulse again, still strong. Then he got up, took a step towards Barbara and grabbed her hand. They stood in silence, staring at the unconscious man on the floor.

"Richard," Barbara whispered when her breathing had returned to a normal rhythm and peace had returned to her face.

"Yes, Barbara?" he asked.

"Thanks."

He squeezed her hand, and they waited for the ambulance to arrive.

Acknowledgments

Columbus Creative Cooperative would like to thank all of the individuals and organizations that made this book possible. It was, without question, the product of many hands.

Thank you to the executive members of Columbus Creative Cooperative. Your insight into each other's work and spirit of collaboration is invaluable.

Thank you to all of the local businesses that have supported Columbus Creative Cooperative in 2011 by retailing our books and sponsoring our work.

Thank you to our editors, Amy S. Dalrymple, Brad Pauquette and Kim Younkin, and a special thanks to Mallory Baker, for her superb proofreading.

Thank you to all of the authors who have ventured into our experiment in local literature.

Finally, thank you, dear reader, for appreciating and supporting local art. With the help of generous patrons like you, Columbus Creative Cooperative can continue to educate and encourage local writers, support local businesses and entertain the fantastic readers of Ohio.

For more information about Columbus Creative Cooperative, please visit **ColumbusCoop.org**.

About Columbus Creative Cooperative

Founded in 2010, Columbus Creative Cooperative is a group of writers and creative individuals who collaborate for self-improvement and collective publication.

Based in Columbus, Ohio, the group's mission is to promote the talent of local writers and artists, helping one another turn our efforts into mutually profitable enterprises.

The organization's first goal is to provide a network for honest peer feedback and collaboration for writers in the Central Ohio area. Writers of all skill levels and backgrounds are invited to attend the group's semi-monthly writers' workshops.

The organization's second goal is to print the best work produced in the region. CCC has printed three anthologies in 2011, and is scheduled to print at least three more in 2012.

The co-op relies on the support and participation of readers, writers and local businesses in order to function.

Columbus Creative Cooperative is not a non-profit organization, but in many cases, it functions as one. As best as possible, the proceeds from the printed anthologies are distributed directly to the writers and artists who produce the content.

For more information about Columbus Creative Cooperative, please visit **ColumbusCoop.org**.

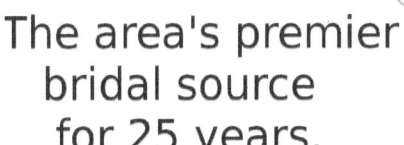

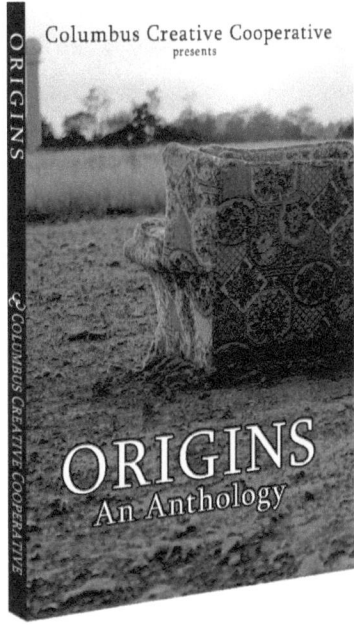